Give Me Tomorrow

KAYE SPENCER

LASTERDAY STORIES, LLC

Give Me Tomorrow
1st Edition short story Copyright© 2007 Kaye Spencer
2nd Edition novelette Copyright© 2018 Kaye Spencer
3rd Edition long novella Copyright© 2025 Kaye Spencer
Cover Design – Livia Reasoner

Published by Lasterday Stories, LLC
www.lasterdaystories.com

All rights reserved.
ISBN: 979-8-9997445-9-3
Library of Congress Control Number: 2025917207

I want you to believe...to believe in things that you cannot.
Bram Stoker
Dracula, 1897

Chapter One

Granger Horse Ranch – Boarding, Conditioning, and Layover Facility
Overland Crossing, Colorado – 1998

Jaxon Granger lurched out of a dead sleep, wide-awake and on the move with the echoes of the emergency buzzer ringing in his ears. Pulling on his jeans, he threw on a flannel shirt over his t-shirt and crammed on his cowboy hat. Alternately hopping on each bare foot, he stomped into his boots then bolted out the front door, his shirt tail flapping in the brisk, early January wind as he raced across the yard.

Bursting through the side door of the indoor exercise arena and stable, he vaulted the metal corral panels and slowed his steps as he crossed to the far side with care so as not to startle the horse his younger brother Steve held by halter and lead rope. Jax approached the horse from the near side, rubbing his hand along the big bay's back as he moved forward with a calming touch.

Bending down, he squinted, grimacing as he inspected the gash blazing across the stud's meaty chest and the lesser slash that went up his shoulder.

"How'd it happen?"

Mac Hartley explained, "I was making the last rounds and found him running loose. He busted up his paddock gate trying to get to a mare."

"Doc Bohlanger coming out, or are we hauling him in?"

"He's in Hawaii at his son's wedding. The new vet working with him is on her way now. She'll assess the injuries and decide."

Jax straightened, pinning Mac with a sharp glare. "She?"

Mac's grin widened.

"Figures."

Mac taunted, "What's your problem? Afraid someday you'll have to give a woman credit for being capable at her job?"

"The last female vet Doc sent out here passed out halfway through the procedure."

Steve argued, "Hey. That was over a year ago. It was August and hotter'n the hubs of Hades that day, and there wasn't a hint of a breeze blowing through this building. We were all feeling it."

"What about Doctor Prim and Prissy last spring? She got herself hurt worrying about her manicure. Doc needs to stop hiring women, and get men who can do the job."

Steve was already shaking his head before Jax finished philosophizing. "I think you'd better reserve judgment with this one. She started working for Doc around Thanksgiving, and she's already in hot demand with horse owners. Seems to be her specialty. I'm surprised she hasn't shown up on your new conquest radar. From what I've heard, she was unattached when she moved here, but that might have changed by now."

"Real funny, Steve. What's her name?"

"M. J. Price."

"I have heard about her. I thought M. J. was a man."

"Maybe she hasn't heard too much negative about you, and she won't think you're a total jackass the minute you open your mouth." Steve jutted his chin to drive his jab home. "You might have a chance to ask her out before she's too jaded toward you."

Jax shot him a go-to-hell look. "You know how I feel about women like her. They have no business trying to do a man's job."

Steve countered, "Trying? Don't you mean doing and succeeding? You didn't think jockeying was for women either, but Allison Keane sure kicked your chauvinistic ass all over the racetrack when she rode Pirate Joe across the finish line in record time last spring. If I recall, you dropped a wad of cash on that race. And lost."

Mac joined in. "You're a pretty good farrier, but I know for a fact that Jackie Burke walks circles around you, and she's a helluva lot prettier. Smells better, too."

"That's right." Steve snapped his fingers, joining in on the fun. "And wasn't it a female orthopedic surgeon who patched you back together when you broke your shoulder? I mean, what's the world coming to? It's downright criminal. Why, women are taking over the very jobs men need to support their families. Who cares if a woman has a family to feed or a husband who's damn glad—and proud—of what she does or makes more money than he does?" He made a histrionic overture of pseudo-alarm. "It's unnatural. Women should stay home. Barefoot and pregnant."

"You two are hysterical." Jax pretended acute interest in the stud's injuries.

Mac added, "Well, none of that ever stops you from wanting to get cozy with them every chance you can."

"Hey, that door swings both ways. Every woman I've dated knew what she was doing, and what she was getting into with me."

"Yeah, but did you know what you were getting into?" Steve poked Jax in the ribs, and Jax batted his hand away. "What exactly happened between you and Allison, anyway? I liked her a lot. She was a keeper. I even heard a rumor you'd bought her a ring. I was looking forward to finally having a sister-in-law and nieces and nephews. Not that the idea of you reproducing isn't the stuff of nightmares." Steve snorted a derisive, grunting laugh.

"Yeah. I want to know, too. What's the deal with Allison?" Mac prodded.

Jax bristled. "Your rumormongers are wrong, and none of your damn business. I didn't buy a ring." He hesitated, knowing full well further comments would dig his hole deeper, but he needed to defend himself. "It was a necklace. For her birthday."

"Diamond?"

"Yeah. So what?"

Mac wiggled his eyebrows. "A diamond necklace is just one piece of jewelry away from a ring."

"Back off. I came to my senses. I didn't give it to her. And I'm not going to."

Mac's deep laughter garnered a middle-fingered response from Jax.

Steve pressed, "I remember the night Allison dumped your ass for good. I was just going back to the house from making the night rounds, and I saw Jackie Burke half-dressed and standing backlit at your kitchen door. You'd stepped out on your deck just as Allison pulled up in her fancy red sports car. She took one look at Jackie and marched right up and punched you in the face. She called you names I'd never heard. Something about unprepossessing misogynistic Neanderthal jerk. You ever look up unprepossessing misogynistic—"

"Shut up, Steve. I know what it means."

"Then you know it fits you like a glove."

"Not that it's any of your business, but there's a little more to the story with Jackie. She was just passing through town, and it isn't what you think you saw. Nothing happened. Anyway, Allison knows the truth about that night. We've made up." He made an offhanded shrug of what's past is past.

"Oh, yeah? When was the last time you talked to her?"

"She sent me a Christmas card. I called to thank her, and she didn't hang up on me."

"You called to thank her. Well, aren't you sensitive and caring? It didn't occur to you that she was reaching out to give you another chance...or third...or fourth—"

"I get the picture. Doesn't matter now. She moved back east where she's got more tracks for jockeying."

Steve shook his head. "You're never gonna change, are you?"

"No, I'm not. I like me just the way I am."

"Well, watch out, because someday a cute little filly will show up and turn your life upside down and inside out. You won't know what hit you."

"Not damn likely."

Dogs barking, then headlights shining through the windows and the sound of tires crunching on gravel interrupted the ensuing guffaws.

Steve handed the lead rope to Jax. "Here, hold him. I'm going out to meet her and welcome her properly. I don't want her to get the wrong idea about me and Mac. You? Well, I don't really give a shit."

Despite his façade of indifference, Jax kept a guarded gaze on the door in anticipation of the first glimpse of this new veterinarian. Always the gentleman, Steve held the door open, and she walked in ahead of him. The sight of the old-fashioned, worn leather medical bag she carried by the handle reminded Jax of an old-timey country doctor making the rounds. Jax looked her over while she listened to Steve's explanation.

Much as he didn't want to admit it, her gender-indeterminate, faded green medical scrubs and scuffed leather work boots meshed with his predetermined expectation of a veterinarian, and he found himself grudgingly approving of what he saw. A visor cap pulled low on her forehead, her ponytail swinging with her steps, along with her round-framed, blue-lensed glasses suggested she was an outdoorsy, but studious, type. He was surprised at the medicinal whiff she exuded when she brushed past him. She didn't marinate in perfume. He glanced at her hands. Trimmed fingernails. No artificial salon-polished nonsense. Another plus to her credit that she didn't feminize the profession. But the question remained, could she get her hands dirty? There was a lot of blood, and the stallion was a handful for a strong man who knew what he was doing.

Walleyed, the stallion snorted as she neared, tugging the lead rope taut, but Jax held him without fighting his head.

"What's his name?" she asked.

"Registered name is Alabama Ike. We call him Ike."

"Hello, Ike. Take it easy, boy. I'm your friend. I'll fix you up good as new." Her voice, soft and soothing, eased Ike's nervousness. "Be patient and trust me, and I'll be done before you know it." She stroked his neck with one hand while holding her other hand palm-up under his muzzle with a compressed alfalfa pellet. He sniffed the pellet then wiggled his lips around the treat and slipped it off her hand and into his mouth.

She continued talking while he nuzzled her clothes for more treats. "I'm Dr. Price. Most people call me Lissa, but I'll also respond to M. J. and Doc. Choose whichever one makes you comfortable."

Steve said, "Oh, sorry. Um, this is Mac Hartley, our foreman, and this goofy bastard ogling you is my brother, Jax. Along with our parents—dad—we own this outfit." Steve hastened to correct himself.

Jax shot Steve a quizzical look, but Lissa spoke and derailed the suspicion forming in his mind.

"Nice to meet you. So, what happened here?" She placed her bag on the ground, opened the center clasp, and brought out a medicinal bottle along with a syringe and needle sealed in a sterile package.

Steve explained, "We weren't expecting to have a mare come in heat just a few paddocks over from his. He tried to pay a visit. We moved her out of range."

Lissa nodded as she peeled the plastic and paper protection from the syringe. "It's not as bad as it looks. A few sutures and salve to help it heal. This time of year, flies and insects won't be much of a problem. Even if a couple buzz around, the salve will stop them from being a nuisance."

"Doc Bohlanger uses staples," Jax said.

"I'm not Doc Bohlanger, am I?" Lissa cut Jax a quick glance as she filled the syringe from the bottle, clamped the syringe sideways between her teeth, swabbed a half-dollar-sized place on the stud's neck with rubbing alcohol, then offered him another alfalfa pellet before she gave him the injection in the dark, damp spot on his neck, which he didn't notice. "I just tranquilized him. Now would be a good time to move him into a fresh stall while it takes effect."

"Already got one ready for him," Steve said.

"Perfect. Can I drive in here so my equipment's handier?"

Already leading Ike toward the stall, Steve said over his shoulder, "Sure, Mac'll open the big doors for you."

Lissa drove her vet truck into the arena and parked in front of Ike's open stall door. A few minutes later, she had everything she needed laid out on the fold-down, horizontal table doors of her mobile vet unit. Attending the horse, she wiped the periphery of the wounds with a disinfectant then injected a local anesthetic along the line of the bloody lacerations.

With Steve holding Ike's lead rope, and Mac stationed in the open stall door as the go-to guy between Lissa and her truck, Jax leaned against the panels, observing her cool efficiency and deft skill with a growing, grudging admiration. She alternated between talking to the horse and humming what sounded like a simple ballad—one of those elusively familiar ballads that plays in the background of old movies. I struck Jax odd that Ike maintained a patient, head-hanging stance, his muzzle occasionally brushing Lissa's shoulder or his breath rustling her hair. It was unlike him. It wasn't just the tranquilizer. There was something more. Something deeper. He couldn't find the right word to describe it. Affection?

Jax waited until she was nearly finished before he spoke. "It's unusual for a woman to go by her initials."

"Is it?"

"What's it stand for?"

"Melissa Jane."

"Ah. Shortened to Lissa."

"Yes."

"Steve says you moved here in November."

"That's right."

Silence.

Jax shifted his weight to his other leg. "Where'd you work before coming here?"

"Thoroughbred racetracks back east. Night shift at emergency vet clinics."

"Where'd you go to vet school?"

"Europe and Scandinavia."

"American vet schools not good enough?"

The head-shaking, eyes-rolling exchange between Mac and Steve wasn't lost on Jax.

"Not at all. American medical universities are excellent. In fact, I have an M.A. in chemistry with an emphasis in blood disorders from a university in Alaska."

"But not your DVM?

"No. The northern European climate was more suited to my health needs at the time."

"You're sickly?"

"It's more of a condition I have to manage."

More silence.

"Been a vet long?"

She paused in the middle of tying the last suture to look at Jax. "Which bothers you the most? My lack of interest in making small talk with you, that I'm vague with my specific credentials, or my gender?"

Steve whistled. "She's pegged you."

Jax ignored him. "Don't get your ponytail in a knot. I'm just curious. I haven't encountered a female veterinarian yet who could do the job as well as a man, let alone better, and there aren't many vets who make middle of the night calls nowadays. You must not have much of a social life."

"That depends upon your definition of a social life. I prefer working nights." Lissa went to her truck and came back with another syringe and a bottle of penicillin. "Keep him quiet for a couple of days then give him light exercise for another week." Handing a tin of salve to Steve, she instructed, "Apply this to the wounds morning and night and any time in between when he's rubbed it off."

"Will do, Doc."

She scratched between Ike's ears while he nibbled alfalfa pellets from her palm. "You'll be all right, fella." With another pat on his neck, Lissa left the stall and went about putting her equipment away. "All right, I'm finished here."

"Thanks, Doc. It was nice to meet you." Mac latched the stall gate.

Steve said, "That goes for me, too. Thanks for coming out. Hope to see you again when it's not an emergency."

"It was nice to meet you both, and I didn't mind coming here at all. Call the clinic if Ike has any troubles. They'll get a message to me through my pager."

"Mac, you and Steve go on to bed. I'll lock up."

"All right, Jax. Goodnight." Steve followed Mac to the arena door.

"Good night," Lissa replied.

"You don't carry a phone?" Jax prodded.

"There's a bag phone in the truck. It's a step up from the radio system. The receptionist at the clinic refers calls to my work number. After hours calls go through a messaging service to my pager."

"Why not one of these?" He showed her his pocket-sized phone. These are the latest technology. Doc Bohlanger carries one just like it."

"Yes, I have a similar phone for personal use and, again, I'm not Doc Bohlanger."

Jax grinned at her reminder. "Why don't you?"

"Why don't I, what?"

"Why don't you take calls on your personal phone or get one of these for work? Seems like responding to a pager wastes time when you could just answer a direct call to a phone."

"I keep my work and private life separate whenever possible."

Jax conceded. "All right. Seems silly to me, but all right."

"You think it's silly, because you're fishing for my personal phone number, and I'm not biting. Any time you want to talk to me, call the clinic. I'll call you back."

Jax just grinned. As he watched her tidy up, his curiosity demanded satisfaction. "Tell me about your health problem. Does it have something to do with your preference of working nights?"

"You're perceptive. I'm sensitive to sunlight."

"Sensitive as in Lupus, or something like that?"

"No. Not Lupus."

"So, what is it?"

Without missing a beat, she said, "Too long in the sunlight and my skin sizzles and sloughs off. It's a nasty sight." She closed a door and walked to the other side of her truck. "It takes a lot out of me to regenerate the damaged skin. I don't care for it."

Jax snorted. "Where did Doc find you? 1-800-DRACU-LA?" He attempted a dramatic and campy Bela Lugosi impersonation that even he realized fell flat, although Lissa came around the back of her vet truck grinning.

"You have more personality than I anticipated."

"Personality? What do you mean?"

"Doc Bohlanger has purposely kept me away from your facility. He wanted me to build up a clientele and a reputation before making my first call out here." She closed the back door of her truck. "He warned me about you."

"What, exactly, did he warn you about?" Jax liked the way her dimples deepened and the sassy turn of her pouty lips when she smiled. He also speculated on what she wore under her scrubs—hoping it was black and lacy—while estimating how many times he'd have to take her to dinner before she slept with him.

"He said you have a poor opinion of career women, which has manifested as a notorious reputation as a lady killer. Consequently, you'll be determined to get me into bed, so you can put another notch on your bedpost."

Jax grunted a *hmmpf.*

"You deny his assessment?"

He shook his head, grinning. "No."

After closing the last door on the vet truck, she added, "He considers you a good friend, and he speaks highly of you, but he also thinks you're heading for a fall."

"What kind of fall?"

"The kind when you fall for a woman you can't have. He said he's looking forward to saying I told you so, and he expects to be a groomsman at your wedding."

"Yeah, yeah, yeah. Doc lectures me every chance he gets." With a glance at his watch, he said, "It's after one. How about an early morning snack? Coffee? Sandwich? Something stronger?"

"Coffee will do. Thanks."

Lissa grabbed the hem of her smock and pulled it up and over her head. He held his breath, hoping to see skin, but wasn't surprised to see a t-shirt that formed nicely to her athletic build. He particularly liked the snug fit of her jeans as she bent over to tug her baggy scrub pants along her hips and off the toes of her boots. He was a leg-man at heart, and the long, lean line of her thighs didn't go unappreciated. Folding her scrubs, she placed them on the front seat, balanced her glasses on the dash, and grabbed her jacket.

"I saw that."

"What?" Eyebrows arched, he faked an innocent grin.

"You finished undressing me. Doc Bohlanger said you'd do that, too."

Half-joking, Jax said, "Dave talks too much. I'll open the doors for you. Drive over to that tan stucco and brick house. I'll close up and be right there."

Satisfied all the doors and stall gates were secure, Jax locked up then walked across the yard under the blue-white glow from the mercury vapor yard lights. He shoved his hands into his jeans pockets and hunched his shoulders against the biting wind and snow flurries. Passing the vet truck, he glanced inside, expecting to see Lissa waiting, but the truck was empty. Maybe she'd gone on inside. Crossing the redwood deck, his hand was on the screen door handle when she spoke.

"We overlook and take for granted that with which we're most familiar."

"Shit!" Jax whirled, searching for the source of the disembodied voice.

Chapter Two

Lissa materialized from the darkness with the ethereal grace of a phantom shadow floating on a night breeze.

"Where the hell were you hiding?" He'd have sworn there was nothing there a second ago.

"I wasn't hiding. I was right here beside the house in plain sight if you'd have only taken the time to see, which isn't the same as looking."

Her face reflected an eerie, bloodless-corpse-aura under the mercury lighting, and the sight sent a shiver scuttling down his spine.

"Something wrong?"

Jax opened the door, shaking off his uneasiness with a dismissing wave. "Naw. It's just these yard lights make you look like something out of a horror movie."

"That's not very complimentary."

"But it's the truth. Apparently, we should have installed the amber sodium lights. They're more flattering." He swept his arm across the threshold. "Come on in where you can't sneak up and scare the hell out of me. Have a seat at the island counter there. I keep coffee on 24/7. I sleep when I can and prowl around when I can't."

"*Hmm*. Me, too." Lissa sat on a high-backed swivel stool and looked around the kitchen, which merged into the living room in the sprawling, spacious fashion typical of ranch-style floor-plans. She picked up a *Daily Racing Form* and glanced through it.

Jax placed steaming mugs of coffee on the island countertop and took a chair across from her. "Do you take anything in your coffee?"

"Just black, thanks."

"Help yourself. I have a sweet tooth with a caffeine addiction. Dark chocolate and coffee is a tasty combination." He pushed a dish of wrapped candies toward her.

Lissa took a piece of candy from the dish. "Yes, it is. Thank you."

"You're welcome."

When he moved his pile of mail aside, a piece of paper covered in a collage of pencil drawings fluttered to the floor. Lissa retrieved it. "Did you draw these?" She blew into her cup then took a sip.

"Yeah. It's a pastime. A hobby."

"They're extraordinary. The detail and scale are remarkable. You should sell them." She placed the paper between them. "You could have a good business on the racetrack. Owners and trainers will pay top dollar for these. Once you build up a portfolio, I have some connections that could get you a showing."

He shrugged. "Never thought of it. I've sketched since I was a kid."

"Are these random images, or is there a story behind them?"

"Well, sort of a story. Last week, I mentioned to my sister-in-law, Mandy, that I've been having a recurring dream for months. She thinks I'm resisting a life message that's trying to make it through my thick head to teach me something." He grunted disdain.

"You sound skeptical."

"Mandy believes dreams have meaning. She reads Tarot cards, and she sees omens and portents everywhere. It's just hocus-pocus horseshit to me."

"Only a fool mocks what he doesn't understand."

"No. It's a fool who doesn't believe in the right here and now. What I see, hear, smell, taste, and touch are real. I'm not mocking. I'm stating fact."

"As you see it."

"Is there another way?"

"So...fate, karma, destiny—call it what you like—plays no part in your life?"

"Nope. I'm the master of my fate and the captain of my soul."

Lissa ran her index finger around the lip of her mug. "What if I told you I've designed my own style of divination?"

"I'd say you and Mandy need to meet. You'll become great friends in your shared nonsense."

When she looked up, what he saw in her eyes stopped his next flippant comment before it came out of his mouth. There was age in that look. Timeless and forever age, with the wisdom of someone so much older than the woman sitting across from him. But there was also sadness that spoke of a deep, lingering heartache.

"For the sake of conversation, what kind of divination did you invent?"

"A type of rune."

"Rune? As in Futhark? Norse runes?"

"Ah, you've heard of them."

"I read a lot. What about these runes?"

"Mine are based on the five classical earth elements."

"Earth, air, wind, fire, and spirit."

"You do know something about divination and elemental magic."

"As I said, I'm well-read. Doesn't mean I believe everything I read."

Lissa smiled. "Well, in that, we are similar."

"Reading has always been a way to make long, sleepless nights bearable."

The tiny lines around her eyes tightened. Her gaze fixed upon a spot on the countertop, her thoughts seeming drawn to some faraway memory. She muttered, "Yes... Darkness. The endless darkness of night..."

"What was that?"

Blinking, Lissa lifted her chin, her gaze focused on his face. "Oh, nothing. I wandered back a few years, that's all. What were we talking about?"

Jax tucked this incident away for revisiting another time. "Your Earth element runes."

"My runes. Yes. When they beckon, I consult them."

"Did they beckon you recently?" He couldn't believe he asked that question with a straight face. What the hell was going on?

"Yes. Three days ago. Then again right after I took the emergency call from Mac."

"And...?"

"And they cast similarly both times—specifically one particular rune that separated itself from the others."

"Coincidence."

She was shaking her head before he finished the word. "No. I don't believe in coincidence. Our decisions, our actions, everything that happens to us leads us toward our destiny. Call them what you will—runes, oracle, tarot, the iChing, tea leaves. If we but open our hearts to their messages and listen with our minds to what these life-guides tell us, we can better understand our being."

"Being?"

"Existence. The meaning of why we're here. What we need to do and learn along our life's path."

"Okay, I'll bite. I'd like to see your runes." He was willing to go along to keep her from leaving.

From her jacket pocket, Lissa withdrew a small stone and held it between her thumb and middle finger for him to see. "I only brought this one."

Jax looked from her hand to her face. "It's a rock."

Her soft, mocking chuckle got under his skin.

"Oh, but it is so much more. Rocks, stones, pebbles. They're timeless. They carry the memories of the ages. When you pick up a rock—not just any rock, but one that catches your attention—and run your fingers and thumb over it and turn it in your palm, it's because that stone senses a connection with you." She went through the motions with the small stone as she explained. "I designed this method of divination for myself during the years I lived with gypsies."

"Gypsies?"

Lissa nodded. "Romanian gypsies."

Jax cleared his throat and shifted in his seat. "Are you serious, or are you just having some fun with me?"

"I'm serious. Dead serious."

Her eyes held the truth of her words, at least as she believed them, which didn't do much to ease his concern that she was about half a bubble off plumb.

"Why just one?"

"Because I pay attention to my instincts and feelings, and this stone told me to bring it with me tonight."

"Why?"

"I don't know why."

Jax cut her a frowning glance. "What good is fortune telling if it doesn't tell you anything helpful?" Still, he held out his hand, and she dropped the quarter-sized stone onto his palm. Rubbing the pad of this thumb over the surface as he turned it over, he said, "It's a flat rock with squiggly marks on both sides. So what?"

"The squiggly marks represent fire."

"As I said, so what?"

"What descriptors come to mind when you think of fire?"

"Heat. Warmth. Light. Cooking. October. Autumn. Bonfire."

"I think you have a deeper imagination."

"All right. Fire is... Anger. Passion. Desire. Death and love. Fire transforms, destroys."

"You're right, but it also creates something new in the ashes."

"Like a Phoenix rising?"

Lissa nodded slowly, her gaze locked on his face, her eyes clouded with that faraway gleam he'd seen earlier. What was in that look? Regret? Longing? Fear? Whatever it was sent a skin-prickling tremor along his arms.

Shaking off the crawling sensation, Jax said, "Making marks on a rock doesn't change the fact that it's an inanimate object. See?" He flipped the rune between his thumb and fingertips. "It feels like a rock." He smelled the rock. "It's odorless like a rock." Then he held it to his ear. "And it's not making any noise... like a rock."

"Aren't you clever? But you left out the spiritual aspect."

Jax put the rune on the table. "It's agnostic. It doesn't care one way or the other."

On a soft laugh, Lissa said, "You are comfortably rooted in reality, aren't you?"

"Yeah. We've exchanged phone numbers."

"We've apparently reached an impasse on this topic, so tell me more about your dream." She tapped the paper. "What about these structures? An obvious commonality is that they're shelters for animals, not humans."

"Sometimes it's a fancy facility like we have here. Most of the time, it's a dilapidated and weatherworn farmstead barn with a hayloft and stanchions and cupolas on the roof. Mandy says I'm looking for a place I can't find."

"What place is that?"

He shrugged. "My place in the world, which she says is why I never dream about a house."

"A house. Not a home?"

"No difference." Jax made an encompassing gesture that took in the kitchen and adjoining living room. "This is my house, therefore, it's my home."

Something in her nod and knowing smile sent him a warning that he was digging himself another hole, and she was getting ready to shovel dirt in on top of him.

"What about this riderless horse? A runaway, perhaps? There appears to be tall grass or weeds that have overgrown a forgotten road."

"You're perceptive."

"Where does the horse come from?'

"It appears out of nowhere and disappears into nowhere."

"Is it always the same horse, and does it travel in the same direction each time you dream?'

"Yeah, it's the same horse, and always just one. It always comes in from the left and keeps going across my line of sight until it's gone in a swirling, murky, misty darkness to the right."

"What about this woman? She appears to be the same woman in each drawing, although her features are indistinct and shadowed."

Jax fixed his gaze and his thoughts on the woman. "She's familiar, yet unfamiliar, if that makes sense, but I never get a good look at her face. She's everywhere, yet nowhere, always watching, elusive and unattainable, and just out of my reach, yet disturbingly enticing." He fell silent, thinking. "Dangerous."

"Dangerous? How?"

Jax's eyebrows pinched together in a hard frown. "Life and death dangerous. But, oddly enough, I'm not afraid of her." He raised his gaze to meet Lissa's intense scrutiny. "And she's strong." Where the hell were these thoughts coming from? He'd never contemplated the woman in his dreams until now. She'd been an image only. Now she was taking on sentient characteristics.

"Strong how?"

"Physically, but also strong in spirit and intellect. She has an old soul. I sense wisdom and immense sadness in her."

"Where are you in your dream? I don't see a likeness of you here."

"I never see myself in the dream. I watch it play out from somewhere separate from the action. I don't know where."

"Does the woman acknowledge you?"

Jax sucked in a sharp breath. "Yeah." Realization rose from the depths of his dreaming memories. "Just before I wake up, she turns a shoulder toward me, but I still can't see her face. I know she smiles, though, like she knows a secret about me."

"Maybe the woman is looking for something in her life, too. Shared dreaming isn't unheard of."

Jax snorted. "Shared dreaming?"

"It's possible."

"Not in my world."

Lissa shook her head, giggling softly. "What else has Mandy said?"

"You're the rune-reader, what do you think?"

Lissa rolled the bottom of her coffee cup in a circle on the bar top. "You don't know who you really are or where you belong, so you're nothing, a nonentity in your dream, which is why there isn't a house. The running horse suggests there's something in your future you must go toward, hence the arrival from the left, or your past, and exiting into the unknown of your future on the right, which is the direction of looking forward." She put the coffee cup down and looked at Jax. "Am I close?"

"Eerily spot-on." Damn, he hated to admit that. He sawed his hand across the back of his neck where the short hairs were standing up. This was getting stranger by the minute.

"How do you feel when you awaken?"

"Feel?"

"Yes. My guess is you feel dissatisfied and often empty, maybe even a little angry for no reason you can pinpoint, but with a yearning for something worthwhile to come along and change your day-to-day routine, although you're not the type to confide that. It's unmanly. I think yours is a life without direction or purpose and, although you have family and acquaintances and probably a handful of close friends, you are, essentially, alone."

Jax opened and closed his mouth on a wordless retort that didn't emerge. There was always a lingering unsettledness when he awoke, but he'd never acknowledged the feelings... until now. She'd taken him to a place within himself he didn't like to visit, and he wasn't about to go there now even if she was dead-center correct.

Shaking off this journey into his well-guarded emotions, he said, "Enough of this nonsense." He stuck the paper to the fridge with a magnet then returned to his bar stool. "Let's get back to something normal. Tell me why you like working nights. The real reason."

"I told you why. Enduring extended periods of sunlight are difficult for me, and there's always something more interesting to do than sleep." Lissa returned the stone to her jacket pocket.

"I agree with you there, but tell me more about your sunlight issue."

"Call it über-photosensitivity."

"That's not a medical condition."

"It sounds more impressive than saying I'm allergic to sunlight."

"Want to tell me about it?"

"Not particularly. Talking about health issues is as boring as looking at pictures of strangers' grandkids."

Jax chuckled. "All right. I get it. None of my business, so I'll change the subject. I noticed you're not only good with your hands, but you also have a way with horses. Ike's not usually that easy to handle."

"He was tranquilized, but thanks."

"No, it was more than that. There was something special, something different in your manner, your touch. And that song you hummed. Sounded like an old ballad. I couldn't quite place it. It sure soothed him."

"It's an old Gaelic song from the Hebrides called 'The Fair Sailor Lad'. I've been around horses all my life. I learned a good long time ago that they respond well to the sound of my voice."

Jax scoffed. "You say that like you've been around for ages. You don't look more than thirty-five or so."

"Forty-one, actually, but I appreciate the compliment. It's been a long and eventful forty-one by ordinary standards. I've aged well, I guess."

The regret in her sigh made him wonder what sadness she carried in her memories. When he lifted his coffee mug, her gaze pinned him with an intensity that stopped his hand. He couldn't look away. She pulled him into her mind, claimed his thoughts as hers, and read what he was thinking. She reached inside his heart and opened the door to his deepest secrets. The room blurred. A crazy thought popped into his head that he was prey to a psychic predator. A shuddering prickle of goosebumps along his arms snapped him back to reality.

Unnerved, he fumbled his cup and tipped his chair in his hasty retreat. "I'm going to check the fire in the other room."

If she replied, he didn't hear her in his flight from the kitchen. With each step from her, his mind cleared. Shaking off the weirdness, he returned to his comfortable world of figuring out how to get her to spend the rest of the night with him. Stirring the coals, he tossed in wadded newspaper and a handful of kindling, blew on the embers, and then added a log to the tiny flames.

Coffee mug in hand Lissa meandered into the living room, drawn to the long gallery wall of framed racing pictures. Everyone who came into the room invariably did the same. It was an impressive collection. The difference was Lissa seemed to appreciate them at a deeper level, for the time it took her to reach the end of the line. Those pictures summed up his entire life, and each one held its own story and memories.

Returning to the beginning, she studied several of the first ones in detail. "This is a remarkable collection of win pictures. It's quite a legacy."

"It is. They're in a general chronological order, top to bottom and left to right."

"I noticed that. I'm guessing you're the taller of the two boys in these earlier pictures, and the cute little guy beside you is Steve. I'd also venture that the man holding the horse is your dad, because the trainer's name is Patrick Granger."

"Right on all."

"Who's the attractive woman in these earlier pictures with you? She's missing in the later ones. There's a family resemblance to you and Steve. Is she your mother?"

Jax resituated the log with the poker and stared into the fire. Peripherally, he saw her watching him, expecting an answer to a reasonable question.

"I'm sorry. Did something happen to her?"

A dry, mirthless laugh rose from a familiar, dark place in his heart, bringing with it the festering hurt. "Yeah, she abandoned us."

Chapter Three

"Abandoned. That's a loaded word. When?"

"I was just a kid. Fifteen."

"Your voice says you're still carrying a grudge."

"You could say that." Jax hooked the poker in the iron tool stand and leaned an arm on the mantel, his gaze scanning the pictorial story of his life spread across the wall. Every time he thought he had a grip on his anger, his hurt and resentment brought it back stronger and blacker.

"Well, I understand about holding a grudge."

Her words, although low and distant, created a moment of shared common ground, and he joined her there.

"What's your grudge?"

"A life and death decision I made a long, long time ago."

"Your life, or someone else's?"

"Mine. I chose to live."

"How was that a bad thing?"

"It wasn't, at least not at the time, and not under the circumstances."

"Why hold a grudge for living? You look healthy. I assume you make a decent living. That's more than a lot of people can say."

"You're right. It is, and I'm thankful for what I have." Her smile belied the sadness darkening her eyes. "It just didn't occur to me at the time how lonely living would be. I'm tired of it."

"Tired of being lonely or tired of living?"

"Yes." She gulped a swallow of coffee then stared into the mug.

Jax cleared his throat. "You weren't...um...you're not...suicidal...are you?" Their common ground turned to quicksand under his feet. This wasn't a place he could stay.

"No, I'm not suicidal. In fact, quite the opposite, I intend to live forever." The self-deprecating chuckle in her voice was out of kilter with her words.

"Don't we all? It's good to have a goal in life." His lame attempt at levity made him even more uncomfortable. "Seriously, though, no one lives forever."

"Forever is longer than you can imagine," she mused. After a moment, she asked, "What's your life's goal?"

This was more to his liking. He knew exactly what he wanted. Walking to her, he took her empty mug and set it on the coffee table. "To kiss as many beautiful women as possible."

"Just kiss?"

Grinning, he said, "Well, kissing is a good place to start. Kissing opens doors to other activity." He slipped her jacket off her shoulders to test how solid his footing was with her. When she let the jacket fall to the floor, it was an invitation he accepted. "Maybe after a kiss or two, you'll consider staying for a while longer."

"Subtlety isn't one of your attributes. You have no idea what you're in for if I stay."

When he slid his arms around her waist, her eyes narrowed, and her pouty smirk egged him on. "Is that a warning or a chall—"

She slammed her mouth against his, stopping his words. Grabbing handfuls of his shirt she backed him up against the rock wall of the fireplace, kissing him as no woman ever had. She snaked her hands under this shirt and planted her palms against his chest, her long, lean body pressing against his. An unnatural heat radiated from her mouth, steaming his senses, warming his blood. Captive to her kisses and roaming hands, a cloudy haze filled his mind. Murky oblivion overtook his control. Something was happening in his head—that same something she'd done in the kitchen. Prey succumbing to predator flashed in his head, yet he was powerless to resist her.

Her tongue traced a path around his ear. Soft lips brushed his cheek. Warm, moist breath caressed his neck with kisses. Unable to keep his eyes open, he sank to the floor with a sense of losing himself to whatever Lissa wanted to do. She straddled him, settling across his belly and bent low over his chest, nuzzling his neck.

"Shit!" A sharp sting brought him roaring back to his senses. Jax slapped his hand to his neck in the instant Lissa leaped off him. "What the hell?" Rising on an elbow, he stared at the blood on his fingers. Slowly, he turned his gaze where she crouched a few feet away, watching him with a wide-eyed feral gleam in her eyes, the back of her hand pressed against her mouth. He swore he saw pearly-white points of fangs against her bottom lip.

"Lissa—"

On the move, she swept up her jacket as she sprinted for the kitchen and out the door. Standing on shaking legs, Jax staggered his way to the kitchen window and peered at her receding taillights until she reached the main road and drove out of sight. Standing there, he inspected his neck in the reflection of the windowpane. A bloody smear, but no marks. Not even a hint of a bite.

"Damn," he muttered. "Damn."

His sketches on the fridge caught his attention when he poured a cup of coffee, and he slipped the paper from under the magnet. He glanced out the window then back at the drawings with the growing realization that the dream woman and Lissa were somehow connected. There was even a slight resemblance. For a couple of seconds, he considered following her then rational thinking returned to remind him he didn't know where she lived, and she was too far down the road to follow now anyway.

Well, come daylight, he'd do some investigating and find out more about this enigmatic woman with a biting fetish. How in the hell did a bleeding bite not leave a wound? Next time he saw her, she had some explaining to do.

Like a jackrabbit running for cover, Lissa spun out of the yard in a spray of gravel in her flight to get away from Jax. She was miles down the road before her nerves calmed enough that she could think. How had he done that? How had just a kiss turned her inside-out? His mouth, burning and possessive. His thoughts pulling her into his mind and drawing forth feelings she believed were as dead as the husband and daughter she'd lost centuries ago. One second, they were sinking to the floor, and the next, the blood pulsing through his carotid artery mere inches from her mouth lured her into the bite before either was ready. The instant she'd tasted his blood, her mind had spiraled into a tailspin of vertigo and vivid memories of her past, which broke her already-tenuous telepathic hold on his mind.

What happened? Even as the question formed, she knew the answer. Those older and wiser had warned that her cavalier indifference toward her victims would catch up with her. Someday she'd meet The One. The man whose strength of mind and will of heart matched—or exceeded—her own. She knew this man from her dreams. He stole into her lonely nights, faceless and ethereally enticing, with a whispered promise of tomorrow on a voice as tender and familiar as the caress of a lover. Only this man could lift the centuries of loneliness from her shoulders and breathe life back into her cold, dead heart.

And now she'd found him...or he'd found her, and he wasn't immortal, not her kind. He was hindered by a finite lifespan. He couldn't go where she traveled.

Moving on to the next job and the next town was her reality, as always, but for the first time, she didn't want to leave. Better judgment argued with her emotions. She wanted another chance with Jax, but that meant explaining, which meant she cared. Caring brought confiding and confiding required trusting, which she had precious little to draw from. The very essence of what allowed her to live also kept her alone and kept her safe.

Suddenly, she was tired. Tired of staying one suspicion ahead of people when they questioned why she didn't age. Tired of concealing what she was. Tired of her nomadic life.

Just plain tired. What good was immortality if she had to endure eternity alone?

Brushing a weary hand over her eyes, she blew out a hard breath. She had no one to blame but herself. Through her own arrogance and apathy toward life, she'd overplayed her hand with Jax. So... What to do now?

She was out nothing but her time—the one thing she had in abundance—if she stayed around long enough to check on Ike in a few days and face whatever Jax had to say. The worst that would happen is he'd tell her she was a freak, and that he never wanted to see her again. She could deal with that. After all, vampire sanctuaries were all over the world, and she'd stayed in each at one time or another. Disappearing and reinventing herself was something she was not just good at, she'd perfected it to a science.

"Hey, Jax! Lissa's coming up the driveway." Steve waved the long-handled grilling fork toward the vet truck coming along the lane. "Looks like you'll have another chance to make a bad impression."

His cackle brought a scolding from Mandy. "Play nice, boys."

Jax shot his brother a frown. "You're a riot."

Beer in hand, Jax left the warmth of the patio fireplace and walked out to greet Lissa amid the menagerie of dogs running about barking their greeting. When she got out of her truck, Jax looked her over as she took several moments to pet the brindle Catahoula, the Jack Russell bouncing like he had springs on his feet, and the old spotted mutt winding in and around her legs as she offered them treats. She was dressed much the same as the other night. Blue scrubs, work boots, and denim jacket. Her hair was pulled up, the ponytail sticking out of the opening in the back of her billed cap. The sight of her energized him with the prospect of finishing what she'd walked out on the other night.

He hadn't learned much about her in his three days of phoning friends at racetracks around the country. Doc Bohlanger knew more than most, and even he was sketchy on the particulars of her background. She had the right credentials for the job, and her references spoke highly of her skills. It was as if she'd taken the essence of the memories people had of her when she left, and all that remained was a shadowy impression.

Steve called out, "Hey, Doc, you're just in time for supper. I've got a steak with your name on it and a cold beer in the fridge."

"Thanks, but can't. I'm on call."

"So, don't have a beer. You can still eat with us."

She laughed. "How about a compromise? Coffee and conversation."

"You got it."

"Good to see you again," Jax greeted.

"Is it?"

"What's that mean?"

"Everything, and then maybe nothing. How's Ike?"

Jax eyed her. "Healing. Let's go have a look."

A couple of minutes of small talk later, they reached the stall. Jax took hold of Ike's halter, while Lissa slipped Ike an alfalfa pellet as she inspected her handiwork.

"Looks good. He's ready for light exercise. Keep it short, but frequent. You don't want him to get restless and rambunctious. Can you remove the sutures, or shall I?"

"You can. That way you'll come back at least one more time."

She patted Ike's neck, and he nuzzled her pockets for pellets. "Is that an invitation strictly for my vet services or for something more personal?"

Jax closed the stall door behind them. "Both. And now that you've brought it up, what happened the other night?"

She shrugged. "I changed my mind."

"That's it? You got me all worked up just to change your mind?"

"Yes. It's my prerogative."

"True, but you don't strike me as a trouser-teaser. You left me in a sorry state and wondering if I'd ever see you again. Are you always mercurial? Hot one minute, cold the next?"

She rocked her head back and forth, considering. "Pretty much."

"There's something wildly enticing about a woman who makes the first move. Especially an aggressive move. Why did you leave in such a hurry? We were just getting a good start."

"We lacked appropriate protection."

Jax crossed his arms, nodding slowly. "I had that kind of protection covered, but I think you mean something else. Something I don't understand." Although she said nothing, the sparkle in her eyes told him he was right. "You bit me."

Lissa pursed her lips and scrunched up her nose in a little cringe. "I did, didn't I?"

"Yeah. You could have warned me. It was a nice touch. It just surprised me. I can handle it rough. In fact, the rougher the better. You should have stayed around. I wouldn't have disappointed."

Her lips pooched into a too-smug smirk. "You don't know what rough is."

"If we find ourselves in a similar situation—hopefully in the not-to-distant future—will you bite me again?"

"Yes."

He caught himself laughing. "You didn't hesitate."

She wiggled her eyebrows. "Biting is my specialty. It adds to the moment. Heightens the pleasure."

"For whom?"

"Me." She shrugged. "I'm a hedonist. I'm all about wanton gratification at the expense of others." She looked him over. "I think we're alike in that aspect. From what I've heard about you, we both use others selfishly for our own pleasure with complete disregard for their feelings."

It wasn't complimentary, but he couldn't disagree. "Okay, I'll give you that. So, from one hedonist to another, when can we try this again?"

Lissa shook her head. "No time soon. Maybe never."

"Why not?"

"Because you can't handle what I've got to offer."

Jax snorted a derisive grunt. "Oh, sweetheart, don't underestimate me."

"You've got a big ego."

"So I've been told." He shot her a sly grin. "There was blood on my neck after you bit me, but there's not a trace of a mark. Explain."

Lissa shrugged. "You must be a quick healer."

"That's not an explanation."

"And yet, it's all you're getting."

Undaunted, Jax pressed her. "To puncture my skin the way you did, you'd have to have razor-sharp teeth. I have a weird picture in my head that right when you jumped off me, there were two shiny-white, pointy teeth pressed against your bottom lip with blood on the tips."

"Pointy teeth, huh?"

The amused skepticism in her voice didn't ring true.

"Yeah, like those plastic Halloween vampire teeth."

"You have a vivid imagination."

"Humor me. Let me see."

Lissa bared her teeth. "Satisfied?"

He chuckled. "No."

She giggled along with him. With a wide gesture, she suggested, "Why don't you show me around before this conversation goes south?"

"All right, but I'm not dropping this. I'm just putting it on hold."

"Trust me. It's best if you just leave it alone."

"For now."

Lissa leveled a frown on him. "You're pushing."

"It's my nature."

"And it's my nature to not let you push me just because you want to."

"Fair enough. Let's go over there."

As they walked, he pointed around the premises. "Mac's house is the stucco and brick opposite mine. No doubt, you figured out Steve lives in that brick ranch-style where he's grilling. That's where we grew up. It's still my dad's house."

"Your dad lives with Steve?"

"No, he runs a string of thoroughbreds in Phoenix. Sometimes, he comes home for a quick visit in the spring, and then he summers here to get out of the Phoenix heat."

They crossed the several yards to another stable with a wide alleyway down the center and went on out through the back doors. Jax stopped to admire the layout. Paddocks or outdoor runs led out from each stall to the fenced pasture beyond where dozens of horses and half as many goats grazed.

"That looks like a full-mile track. I don't see a starting gate in the chute extension on the backside. That surprises me since you do conditioning here."

"It is a mile track." Jax gazed at the track spread out on the flat beyond the two hot walkers enclosed in round pens near the wash rack. "We've got a new starting gate on order—all the latest bells and whistles."

"There's a half-mile track at the place I'm renting. Weeds and grass have overgrown it, and the fence is in sorry shape."

Jax perked up. "Oh, yeah? In a few months, I'm going to trailer some colts to a training track about an hour away to give them a different experience. I'd rather stay closer to home. I'll drop by your place and take a look. Maybe it's worth fixing up. I've lived around here all my life, so I might know some history of it. Where do you live?"

"Nice try."

He feigned innocence. "What? If you don't want me to know where you live, why did you offer the track?"

"It wasn't an offer. It was an observation for the sake of conversation. The track isn't usable."

"Why not let me judge that?'

"Not a good idea."

"You know I'll find out where you live."

"Not until I want you to know."

"When will that happen?"

"No time soon."

"You said that before."

"And I meant it both times." Gesturing, she asked, "The tractor-trailer outfit over there. Transport?"

Grinning at her deliberate change of subject, Jax said, "Yeah. We haul all over the country. One of our two drivers retired a month ago after hauling for us for ten years. We haven't found a hirable replacement."

"I'll bet it's difficult to find a decent driver who also understands horses. You have to have the right person, or you're asking for a horse to get hurt."

"That's why either Steve or I will pick up the slack until we find someone."

"Hey, you two! Supper's on." Steve waved them in.

"On our way!" Jax yelled back.

"Then kick it in gear. We're hungry."

Jax cut a sidelong glance at Lissa. "My little brother has always been a bossy brat."

Giggling, Lissa asked, "Is he your only sibling?"

"Yeah."

"You seem close."

"We are. Best friends."

"You're fortunate to have someone like that in your life. Do you have other family nearby? Grandparents? Cousins? Aunts and uncles?"

"Both sets of grandparents are living. My dad's parents—Sue and Kevin—live in town. Marilyn and Rod, my mo— My other grandparents live in Phoenix. They travel a lot, so they come through here several times a year to spend time with Steve's kids. I've got aunts and uncles and a few cousins here and there. Some live just down the road." Jax glanced at her. "What about you? Where's your family?"

"I have none."

"None?" Jax stopped. "That's impossible. Everyone has someone."

"Not everyone."

"Seriously? You don't even have cousins?"

"No. I have no living relatives." Lissa walked on a few steps then turned to face him. "What you really want to know is if I'm unattached. We sort of skipped that in the introductions."

"Yes, we did. Steve's under the impression you're single, but I want to know for myself."

Lissa's eyes shone with remembered sorrow. "I was married."

"Was married? Divorced?"

"He died."

"I'm sorry. That's rough. Kids?"

On a slow nod and soft, wistful words, she said, "A daughter. Juliet." Raw pain in a flash of memories passed over her face, and her shoulders heaved on a deep breath that she exhaled on a head-shaking sigh. "It's been years, and it's still hard to talk about her. She died a year before her father died." She walked on toward Steve's house, abruptly ending the conversation.

"Damn." He didn't know what else to say, so he said it again. "Damn." After a few seconds, he followed her.

Lissa accepted the cup of coffee from Mandy as Steve made introductions.

"Mandy, this is the vet I've told you about—Lissa Price. Doc, this is my gorgeous and sexy wife, Mandy. The three rug rats running around are Jake, Marci, and Lindsey. Every morning I wake up and ask who they are and why they're calling me Daddy, but Mandy swears they're all mine."

"Oh, shush." Mandy smacked Steve on the arm. Holding out her hand to Lissa in welcome, she said, "I'm so pleased to meet you. You'll have to ignore Steve and Jax. They think they're witty and charming."

Bewildered, Steve looked between Mandy and Jax. "Aren't we?"

Mandy laughed as she helped toddling Lindsey climb onto her lap. "No, you're not, but I love you two rascals, anyway."

As dishes went around the table, Steve said to Lissa, "Mandy's sort of in your line of work."

"Oh? What work do you do?"

"Equine chiropractor. I also do equine massage."

"That's good to know. Massage is becoming increasingly popular among horse owners. Show horses as well as racehorses. I'll keep you in mind. Do you have business cards?"

"Yes. I'll give you some before you leave."

Lissa felt at home amidst the Granger family and Mac with their easy laughter and endless racetrack stories. Some two hours of conversation later, she was disappointed that her pager went off.

"Excuse me. I need to check this." She made the call on her mobile phone then returned to the patio. "Dog versus porcupine. I have to go. The conversation was great. Thanks."

Steve pointed the neck of his beer bottle at Jax. "You've been pleasantly mute tonight. Think you can keep it up and walk her to her truck without annoying her? In spite of you, we'd like to see her again."

"Shut the hell up, Steve."

Jax accompanied Lissa to her truck, opened the door, and she slipped behind the steering wheel. It amused her that Jax carefully positioned himself in the open door with his right forearm resting on the roof.

"Thanks for staying."

"You have a wonderful family. The kids are delightful. I enjoyed visiting with everyone." Right foot on the brake, she depressed the clutch with her left and turned on the ignition switch.

"What are you doing Saturday morning? Say around seven. We're galloping two- and three-year-olds. Should be some fine entertainment. It wouldn't hurt to have a vet on-site. Seems like one of the silly things always gets hurt the first couple of times out in a group."

"I'll see what I can do."

Jax smiled and leaned inside the cab, his intent clear.

She stopped him with a firm hand against his chest. "Don't."

"Why not?"

"It's not a good idea."

"Oh, but I think it is." He planted a solid kiss on her mouth and snaked his tongue between her lips as she let out the clutch.

"Goodnight, Jax."

Pulling away, Lissa looked in her side mirror at Jax watching her drive away, his silhouette illuminated by the mercury light. She licked her lips to catch the memory of his kiss. He was a bad boy. She knew it, but the combination of his self-assured masculinity, baby blues, and the way he smelled of horses, barn dust, leather, and liniment sent a shiver down her back.

Turning onto the asphalt, she sighed. Over the years, she'd met all manner of men from aristocrats to professors and indentured servants to pirates. She'd enjoyed them for the pleasure and sustenance they provided, but she'd never wanted more. When it was time, she'd simply left them and never regretted leaving.

And look at her now. How had she let this happen? How had she let Jaxon Granger blindside her? It was going to be a long night trying to keep her mind on extracting porcupine quills and not on anticipating seeing Jax in a few days.

Chapter Four

Saturday morning, Lissa turned off the main road and onto the graveled, poplar-lined driveway at the sign directing her to the Grangers' headquarters. She smiled at the first warning sign:

Private Property.
Trespassers will be shot.
Survivors will be violated.

She grinned again, halfway down the lane, at the next sign that read:

Old dogs. Young dogs. Several stupid dogs.
Please drive with care.

She liked the Granger brothers' dry humor.

Parking at the arena, she walked on past the paddocks to the rail fence around the perimeter of the track to watch the half-dozen riders and horses galloping in a close bunch. Jax yelled a greeting as he breezed by. The group pulled up on the backside, and by the time they reached her again, they'd brought their young horses to slow, cooling trots.

On this pass, Jax pulled up and flipped his goggles up over his helmet brim. "You ever do any galloping, Doc?"

"Yes, but not in a couple of years. Why?"

"Take one out with me." His colt pulled at the bit to catch up with the others, and Jax gave him his head to follow.

Lissa met Jax at the far end of the arena, which served as a combination barn, stable, and indoor exercise area just as he jumped off his mount at the open doors and handed the horse over to a groom.

He looked her over as he walked up. "Nice to see you in broad daylight."

"Long sleeves, leather gloves, hat, and sun barrier lotion. I'm good for a few hours."

Jax grinned. "Then let's not waste time standing here. Long night at the clinic?"

"Not too long. A big dog met a little porcupine with a bad aim."

Mac called from inside, "Ready for another one?"

Jax removed his helmet and held it in the crook of his arm, then ran his hand through his wavy hair. Over his shoulder, he said, "Yeah. Bring two out. And another helmet."

"Got it," Mac said.

Mac and Steve appeared with a sorrel filly and a chestnut colt. Lissa took the filly and checked over the tack. She tightened the girth on the flat saddle, gave the stirrup leathers a quick measure, and shortened them each a notch. Tugging the helmet down on her head, she buckled the chinstrap.

"You've obviously done this a few times."

"A few."

"It's a fast track this morning. Dry and even."

Mac gave Jax a leg up. Although smiling, Mac grumbled, "Damn well better be. I worked on it all day yesterday."

Steve held the bridle and boosted Lissa to the filly's back with his free hand. She took up the slack in the reins as the horse stepped out. Steve led her to the track, and Mac followed with Jax's colt. Steve drew the pole closed across the gap once Lissa and Jax took off for the walk-trot, limber-up round.

Jax jerked his head toward the crowd gathering at the rail. "We've got spectators. We have a rule that only employees can exercise the horses. Not even the owners, trainers, or jockeys."

"So, they're all wondering how I managed to get around that." Lissa cast a chastising smirk his way.

He laughed. "Boss's prerogative. And I'm the boss today."

Stirrup to stirrup, they broke into a slow canter.

"It's been awhile since I've been on a flat saddle. I hope I don't disappoint them."

"Not likely. You ride like a pro. Where have you galloped?"

"Chicago, Cleveland, Louisville, Penn National—to name a few in America."

"America? Meaning you've ridden in other countries?"

Lissa just smiled, arrogant in her silence.

Chuckling, Jax replied, "Remind me that I want to hear more about that. Right now, we'll do a slow mile while they get their legs under them. Keep them together."

The filly tugged at the bit, but Lissa kept her in check with Jax's colt.

Finishing the mile, Jax called to her, "This time, let her have her head. Think you can handle blowing her out down the stretch?"

"The real question is, can *you*?"

As they came around the far turn, Lissa laid low over the filly's neck and urged her on. The little sorrel stuck her nose out, stretched her neck, and left Jax a length behind as they raced along the backside then hugged the inside rail around the clubhouse turn. Jax caught the filly coming out of the turn, and the two horses thundered neck and neck down the straightaway to the home stretch.

Fifty feet from the imaginary finish line, Lissa let out a rousing yell, and the filly surged ahead to beat Jax by half a length. Standing in her stirrups and tugging on the reins stiff-armed to brace herself against the filly's momentum, Lissa eased the young horse into a canter then a trot, and finally a cooling, prancing walk.

Jax fell in beside her. "Not bad for a lady vet."

"Not bad for a conceited, chauvinistic cowboy."

He grinned. "Do you have time for another go?"

"Only if you're willing to be outrun again."

He laughed. "Bring it on."

At the barn, Steve and Mac took hold of the horses' bridles as Jax and Lissa jumped off.

"Damn, Doc. That was good," Steve said. "It's about time we got someone here who knows what the hell they're doing on the back of a horse." He cut a sidelong grin at Jax.

"Thanks. I'm taking that as quite a compliment." From the corner of her eye, she caught Jax flipping Steve off. Smiling at their good-natured bantering, she liked this new experience of humans as friends and not as a source of sustenance.

On the next trip around the track, her pager went off. "Gotta take a call," she yelled and pointed back to the arena. They finished the run, returned the horses to Mac and Steve, then Jax accompanied her to her vet truck while she made the call.

"Doc Bohlanger needs me at the clinic. Thanks for the rides. I haven't done that in a long time. I enjoyed it." Lissa slid onto the seat, closed the door, and rolled down the window as she started the motor.

"I'm glad. How about dinner tomorrow night? Seven-thirty?"

All the reasons to refuse were unconvincing next to how much she wanted to accept.

"You know you don't have a decent excuse to say no."

If he only knew the truth, he'd think otherwise. "Where?"

"The Colonial."

"Ooh, nice. I haven't been there, but I've heard it's elegant and formal."

"Got a pen?"

She reached into a cup holder and handed it to him.

He took the pen and her hand in the same grasp. Turning her palm up, he said as he wrote, "This is my number." Releasing her hand, he poised the pen over his palm. "What's yours, and where do you live? I'll pick you up."

Lissa glanced at the number written on her hand, then lifted her gaze to meet his. The hope in his eyes dimmed with her hesitation, and he stepped back. So, Jaxon Granger wasn't quite the tough guy he made himself out to be. That was something she understood—the constant vigil of keeping up barriers to protect your heart from disappointment. She knew all too well the secret, silent longing for companionship that battled the self-denial of not wanting or even needing it.

"Tomorrow's out. I'll be at the 4-H horseshow. It'll be a long day of checking health certificates and just being on hand to take care of any injuries."

"That's not a no." The twinkle in his eyes returned. "There are other Saturdays. Pick one."

Letting out the clutch, she said, "I'll check my schedule. Ask me again sometime."

Steve slowed at the crossroads at Clayburn's Corner and turned toward home. Jax caught sight of Lissa's vet truck parked by the barn and craned his neck for a better look.

"Steve. Pull in. Something's going on. Doesn't look good. Lissa's running toward the house."

"I see that."

"What the hell? She just jumped into the well-pit."

Steve pulled into the yard, and Jax got out of the pickup before the tires stopped rolling. Eleven-year-old Roxanne Clayburn ran up to them

"Hurry! Rusty and Thunder fell in the well. Dr. Price is down there with them."

"Who's Thunder?"

"Rusty's Welsh pony."

"Is Rusty hurt?"

"Dr. Price said he's banged up."

"How'd it happen?"

With gesticulation that expressed her I-can't-believe-I-have-such-a-stupid-little-brother, she explained on the run, "I was practicing my obstacle trail course in the arena, and Rusty was doing his own little made-up course out here in the yard. All of a sudden, he yelled, 'Mom. Look at me. I'm king of the hill' and they fell in."

"Jax! Steve! Thank heavens you're here." Nancy Clayburn's due-any-day pregnancy gave breathiness to her words and a flush on her cheeks.

Jax dropped to his knees beside Nancy at the edge of the twelve-foot-square dirt-bottom well pit and assessed the situation: Lissa in a corner and holding a whimpering boy; pony pawing and snorting in his rising panic; the wooden rung ladder once bolted to the wall now in pieces; pipes and conduit running here and there; pump jack on a concrete slab just off center.

From down in the pit, Lissa's voice rang out clear. "Turn off the electricity!"

"Where's the breaker box?" Steve asked.

Nancy waved toward the house. "Back porch. West wall. Breakers are clearly marked."

Steve took off.

Lissa called out again, "Jax, I need help. I'm pinned between the pony and the pressure tank."

"I see that. I'll come down. How's Rusty?"

"Lacerated scalp and bloody lips and nose. Might be broken. He's a trooper, though. Hasn't cried."

Jax eased himself down into the well all the while talking in a soft tone. "Easy there, Thunder. Easy." He laid a hand on Thunder's rump to let him know he was there.

Steve returned and peered into the pit. "Where's Bill?"

Nancy said, "He went to the lumber yard for more materials for the new well cover. He'll be back any time now. He laid planks across the top and warned Rusty to stay away, but he obviously paid no attention."

Steve consoled her, "Kids and ponies are naturally drawn to mischief, and boys are born without impulse control. It takes them longer than girls to figure out they need to think before they do boneheaded things."

"Yeah, like twenty-five years or so," Jax mumbled.

Roxanne piped up, "Tell that to Dad. He's going to tan Rusty's hide once he finds out he's okay."

"Roxie, be nice," Nancy scolded. "He'll do no such thing."

Jax said, "We'll need a loader tractor and chains—"

"The farmhand is down the road at the hay shed. There are chains on it. I'm not much good to you here with this baby tummy in the way, but I can drive a tractor." Steve helped Nancy to her feet. "Roxie, do what you can to help." Nancy went to her car.

Jax maneuvered around the pump jack for solid footing. "Rusty. I want you to slide across the saddle and grab hold of me."

Lissa guided Rusty to make the transfer, then Jax swiveled and faced the wall right below Steve. "Now, pretend I'm a ladder and climb right up on shoulders. That's it. Climb. I've got you. Steady. Use the toe of your boots against the wall. Good. Now, reach for Steve."

"Gotcha!" Steve hauled Rusty up and out over the cinderblock-tall lip at the top of the pit. "Roxanne, take him inside and call Mandy. Tell her what happened. She'll come right over."

Thunder reached his limit and tried to rear, but he couldn't get enough lift in the cramped area, so he threw his head. The blow knocked Lissa against the wall, and he came down on her foot with a front hoof.

"Pull him your way! Pull him over!" Lissa pushed Thunder's shoulder and Jax tugged the saddle until Thunder shifted his weight enough for Lissa to extract her foot. Jax cringed right along with her. He'd been stepped on enough times that he didn't need to ask how badly that hurt.

"Tranquilize him?" Jax asked.

"No. No. I can calm him." Lissa took a firm grip on Thunder's bridle to keep his head steady while stroking him with her other hand. "*Sshhh*. Take it easy," she crooned. She dug into her pocket and brought out an alfalfa pellet that the pony sniffed, then nibbled off her palm.

Jax tuned half an ear to the sound of a vehicle pulling up and the indistinct voices that came steadily closer and the other half to Lissa and her soft humming. He recognized it as the song she's hummed to Ike. A shadow fell over them, and they looked up and into the faces of Bill Clayburn and Steve.

"Steve filled me in. How's the pony?" Bill asked.

"Okay, but not any happier to be down here than we are," Jax said.

"I'll bet you're right. I'll run the tractor once Nancy gets here with it. So, we need to rig up a sling."

"Yeah, chains and a piece of tarp or canvas—"

"No," Lissa interjected. "A canvas and tarp won't allow for distributing his weight around his belly. He'll wobble and slip out, especially if he fights us on the way up. We can't chance dropping him."

"Then what do we use? We can't tie ropes around him. They'll cut into him."

"Two stock saddle cinches. One around his girth and the other at his flanks. We'll hook chains to the cinch rings and lift him out. The cinches will hug his body, and keep him more or less level. Trust me on this. I've seen it done."

Jax nodded. "Good enough. I'm game. Bill? Steve?"

"Always follow the doctor's advice." Although light-hearted in tone, there was respect in Steve's voice.

Bill said, "It's worth a try. I'll get the cinches."

"Just one," Lissa said. "We've already got the cinch on this saddle." She looked at Jax. "Do you have enough room to get the saddle off and unhook the cinch?"

"Already working on it."

"Mandy's here. Be right back," Steve said.

Steve and Bill returned at the same time, and Bill dropped the cinch to Jax.

"Now who's here?" Jax asked when he heard the sound of more vehicles.

Bill looked over his shoulder. "Looks like half the county's coming. Who's that?"

"Granny Deacons," Steve said.

"I didn't know she still had a driver's license," Bill complained.

"She probably doesn't." Steve chuckled.

Bill groused, "Erv Johnson. Harry Brown. The Bergman twins. I don't recognize some of the cars. How the hell did word spread so fast?"

Steve laughed. "Party line. Granny Deacons was undoubtedly listening when Roxanne called Mandy."

"Nancy swears this is the busiest intersection in the county. I believe her now."

"Heads up!" Jax handed the saddle up to Bill.

Jax watched Lissa, lost in her own little world with Thunder, marveling at her total focus to keep him calm. Turning his gaze skyward, Jax saw occasional shadows of people moving about and faces of curious people peering down to see the uncommon sight of a pony in the bottom of a well. A few people asked if there was anything they could do, while others just made a peek to appease their curiosity. When the tractor finally arrived, he checked the time. Thirty minutes since he'd jumped into the pit. It seemed a lot longer than that.

Nancy leaned over the edge. "Bill took over. How's it going?"

Jax gave her a thumb's up, but the droning din of the tractor engine drowned out her response. The bucket lowered with Steve astraddle the forks. He guided Bill with gestures until the tractor arms rested on the cinderblocks. Steve fed chains to Jax, and he and Lissa made quick work of securing them to the cinch rings.

Jax yelled, "Take up the slack."

Steve motioned to Bill. The chains went taut.

Steve bellied down on the forks, and called to Jax, "Ready for lift-off?"

"Slow. Don't want to lose him."

"Got it." Steve gave an up signal to Bill.

The chains jerked, and Steve motioned for Bill to continue. Jax boosted Lissa up the wall toward the reaching hands that hauled her out, and he followed right behind her. The bucket-forks raised, and the arms extended as it lifted. Thunder's ears, then his head, cleared the pit. He knew people had gathered, but he was still surprised at the size of the crowd. No one spoke as all attention hung on the pony dangling in the air like a gigantic wasp.

Jax yelled, "He's clear!"

Bill put the tractor in reverse and eased away. Lissa crouched under the forks, just out of danger of Thunder kicking or striking, but prepared to move in as soon as it was safe.

"That's good" Jax made a thumb's down gesture, and Bill let the bucket down until Jax waved for him to stop when Thunder's feet touched the ground. Steve jumped out of the bucket and helped Jax unhook the chains from the cinch rings. Bill waited for the all clear then backed up and parked the farmhand.

Thunder gave a mighty shake as if leaving his ordeal behind, and cheers went up. Lissa checked him over for injuries. Rusty ran ahead of his mom, Mandy, and Roxanne and tried to hug Thunder one-armed while keeping the towel-wrapped ice pack pressed against his nose.

"Is he okay?" Rusty asked Lissa.

"Yes. Superficial scrapes. Skinned shins and hocks, but he's fine."

"Glad you two are all right but, damn, son, you're going to be the death of me with your shenanigans. We'd better get you to the hospital." He tapped the tea-towel wrapped bandage Mandy had put over the laceration on his scalp.

Steve offered, "I'll put Thunder in the corral."

"I'll come along with you," Mandy said.

"Thanks. And thanks, Doc. Jax. This might have turned out differently if you three hadn't been here."

"Glad to help," Jax said.

Lissa knelt to Rusty's six-year-old eye level. "You had a close call. Promise me you'll learn from it. No more acting without thinking first. Okay?" She held her hand up, and he high-fived her.

"Promise."

On-lookers and neighbors dispersed amid a string of *good job, glad it worked out, never saw anything like that.*

"How's your head?" Jax asked as the last car left the yard.

"Fine. Why?"

"When Thunder hit you with his head, the back of your head smacked the wall." He checked through her hair. "Not even a bump. *Hmm.*" He took hold of her hand and led her to the cinderblocks at the top of the well. "Come over here."

"Jax. I'm all right."

"Sit down. I want to see your foot." Jax pulled off her boot bearing the scuffs of a horseshoe. "I expected to dump out a boot full of blood. I could tell by the look on your face how bad it hurt." He peeled off her sock. "There's nothing. No bruising or swelling. I figured at the very least, your toes were broken. Explain that."

Before she could respond, Steve and Mandy walked up. "You're hurt?"

"No. Jax is mother hen-ing me. Thunder was nervous, and it was tight quarters down there. He bumped me a couple of times. I'm all right." Lissa put her sock and boot back on.

"Well, I'll say this for you, Doc, you never cease to amaze me with the things you know about animals and your way with horses. I've never seen anything like it."

Jax smiled. Just about everyone watching had made that same comment, and he agreed with them.

"Maybe it's because I really love what I do."

"Whatever it is, you and Jax make a great team under pressure."

"Yes, you do," Mandy agreed.

Jax grunted a chuckling response, "Maybe we'll go into the kid- and pony-rescuing business." He noticed Lissa ducked her chin and her cheeks seemed unusually rosy.

"I'll catch a ride home with Mandy. Keys are in the pickup."

"I'm right behind you," Jax said. He sat beside Lissa, took off his hat, scrubbed his fingers through his hair, then put his hat back on. "Steve's right, you know."

"About what?"

"You've got a special gift with horses that's uncanny. There's something mysteriously intriguing about you. The more I'm around you, the more I want to know, but the more you don't want to tell."

"Argentinian Malbec wine complements a medium rare sirloin."

It took Jax a few seconds for her meaning to soak in. He cocked his head and eyed her, not sure what to make of her statement. "Are you asking me out on a date?"

She made a noncommittal shrug, but her lips curled into a playful smirk. "Maybe."

"When?"

"Tomorrow night."

"The Colonial?"

"Where else? It's the best steakhouse in a hundred miles."

"Seven-thirty?"

Lissa smiled and nodded.

"It's a date." Jax stood and offered her a hand up. "Can I help with what you were doing before Rusty took the plunge?"

"No. I'd just finished putting everything away. I need to go to the clinic and restock the truck."

"All right. See you tomorrow night." Jax got into Steve's pickup and headed home with his heart as full as the wide smile spreading across his face.

Chapter Five

Jax arrived at the Colonial at seven and took a table in a back corner where he could watch the front door and the parking lot through the plate-glass window. Nursing a beer, he observed the patrons coming and going, while trying not to rubberneck every time a car pulled into the parking lot. By seven forty-five, and still no Lissa, he ordered another beer. He told himself she'd have called if she couldn't make it. Surely, she wouldn't stand him up, especially since she'd initiated the dinner date.

But a little part of him didn't quite believe it. It wasn't that he didn't trust her; he didn't doubt at all that she was good for her word. There was a niggling, out-of-reach something about her that defied explanation or, for that matter, understanding. Whatever it was, he couldn't shake off his need—maybe growing obsession—to know more about her.

A party of ten gathered in the doorway while waiting for a table, which obstructed his view for several minutes. His niggling doubts that Lissa wasn't coming escalated into impatient anticipation. When the waitress finally led the group to their table and the bottleneck in the doorway cleared, Jax expected to see Lissa behind them.

His heart sank. She wasn't—

No! There she was. Standing, Jax watched her, mesmerized at the sight of her form-fitting, low-cut red cocktail dress split up one side with thigh-high black nylons revealing the provocative peek of a garter strap with each flaunting, black-stilettoed step. Her blood-red lipstick accentuated the rosy blush over her cheekbones, and her straight hair, hanging loose to her shoulders, shimmered with sparkling highlights.

"Hello, Jax." Lissa placed her evening clutch beside her plate.

"Good evening." He seated her then resumed his seat, still marveling at the transformation from Lissa the veterinarian to Lissa the woman.

Her eyes shone with an amused gleam. "You're staring."

"You're...absolutely...stunning."

"Thank you. You cleaned up nicely yourself. I didn't picture you as a suit and tie sort of guy."

"I'm not, but when I need to I can, uh, rise to the occasion, so to speak."

A smirk played at her mouth. "Yes, I noticed your...um...rise that night back in January in your living room."

"Glad you noticed."

"Impossible not to."

"We've never pursued that night or even talked about it much."

"And we're not going to talk about it now, either."

Jax chuckled. "Understood. We'll stay on neutral ground tonight."

"Good."

"I stopped at the Clayburns' on the way here. Rusty and Thunder are doing fine."

"Yes. I took them a dozen doughnuts this morning. Rusty was quite proud of the six stitches in his scalp and his black eyes. Thankfully, no broken nose."

"I also researched that old Gaelic ballad you're always humming— *The Fair Sailor Lad*."

"And?"

"I expected a cheerier tune. It doesn't have a happy ending."

"No, it doesn't."

"Want to tell me about it?"

"No."

"Someday?"

"Maybe."

"Not a neutral topic?"

"No."

Jax nodded. "All right." He picked up the open wine bottle. "May I?"

"Please."

He filled their glasses halfway then placed the bottle to the side.

Lissa lifted her glass, swirled the wine, held the glass at chin level, and sniffed. She sipped and held the wine in her mouth for a few seconds before she swallowed. She closed her eyes on a soft, satisfied "*Ummm*."

A waiter took their order, and Jax sat back, wine glass in hand. "So, I did okay with the wine?"

"Excellent choice. Argentinian Malbec has yet to disappoint me."

"What's so special about Malbec?"

"Malbec has ripe blackberry and plum flavors reminiscent of rich jam, not overly fruity, yet sweet enough for a pleasant aftertaste that leaves a sense of rustic, earthy-wood lingering in your mouth."

On a respectful nod, he said, "Well, you know a lot more about wine than me. I'll pay close attention to your observations to learn the finer points."

"It's one of my interests. I've purchased exceptional bottles and vintages over the years."

"So, you're a collector of wine."

"And other artifacts."

"Such as?"

"Rare art and manuscripts. A few documents and musical compositions."

"You haul valuable art and papers along with old bottles of wine around with you from place to place?"

"No. I own property with a specially designed vault that preserves the integrity of the items."

"Where is this mysterious property?"

"Not in America."

"Obviously someone handles the details for you."

"Yes. I retain the services of a law firm that manages such transactions on my behalf."

Jax's eyebrows shot up. "That's intriguingly vague."

"Sorry. That's as specific as I'm willing to offer."

"All right. I'll leave it alone. For now. Tell me more about your rare art and manuscripts. What do you own?"

She watched the wine swirling in her glass.

"Your silence means it's none of my business. If you're not going to explain, then stop throwing out teasers to get my curiosity up."

"Oh, it's not that at all. I hesitate to tell you, because you won't believe me."

"Try me."

Lifting her gaze, she studied him for some time. "All right. An example of a wine I own is a bottle of 1945 Domaine de la Romanée-Conti Romanée-Conti."

"What's so special about it?"

"It's vintage, for one. 1945. It signifies the end of a war. The wine itself was made from ungrafted vines that were pulled up and destroyed. No more can ever be made."

"That is a rare wine. What else?"

"For art, I have Da Vinci's painting of Leda and the Swan. The art world believes it was destroyed. The last record of its existence is in 1625."

"And you just happened to find it?"

"No, but I am its keeper now."

"Hmm."

"Shall I continue, or have you heard enough?"

"No. Go on. This is ludicrously intriguing."

"You're mocking me."

"Sorry. It's my nature. Keep going."

"All right. In the literary realm, I own the manuscript of a presumably lost play, *The History of Cardenio*, which is accepted in scholarly circles as a collaboration between William Shakespeare and John Fletcher."

Jax dipped his chin. "You have a verified lost Shakespearean play?"

"Yes. I wouldn't say I did if I didn't."

Jax nodded slowly, his rational mind telling him this wasn't possible. "Okaaaay... Go on."

"I have a complete and in-pristine-condition Gutenberg Bible, Volumes One and Two, printed on vellum."

"I happen to know there are only about fifty surviving Gutenberg Bibles, and only a few are complete, let alone in good condition. A preserved one would be quite a thing to own. What's the going price at auction?"

"The most recent estimate from my attorney is thirty-five million."

He had no words. It was impossible. But he found no lie in her eyes. Still, he shifted in his chair.

"You're uncomfortable."

"Yeah. I am. Delusional people are champion liars, because they absolutely believe their fabrications."

"So there's no possibility that what I've said is true?"

"I suppose anything's possible."

"Shall I go on?"

Chuckling softly, he said, "Sure, why not?" He leaned back and waved a beckoning hand for her to continue. "What else do you have stashed away in your secret dungeon?"

"Vault. It's a controlled environment that regulates temperature, humidity, and light."

Her put-on frown and pseudo scolding made him chuckle again.

"So, in this vault...?"

"Are you familiar with the composer, Johannes Brahms?"

"Passingly."

"According to many historical accounts, Brahms destroyed much of his early compositions by burning them. He was merciless in his self-criticism. However, unbeknownst to Brahms, an acquaintance salvaged a violin sonata before it burned and held onto it until after Brahms died."

Jax freshened Lissa's wine glass. "And you have that sonata?"

"Thank you. In fact, I do. Now, the item I treasure most is the letter in Ludwig van Beethoven's own hand in which he identifies, by name, his Immortal Beloved." She took a sip of wine.

"No."

"Yes."

"That's incredible. Historians have spent...what...a hundred-and-fifty years speculating about the woman's identity."

"One hundred sixty-three years to be precise." She smiled over her wine glass, her eyes sparkling with mischievous delight at his bewilderment. "You clearly doubt me."

"Yeah. I do. You're either a card-carrying pathological liar or just plain nuts."

"There's a third possibility?"

"That you're telling the truth."

Lissa nodded.

Jax gulped a swallow of wine. "Because I don't want you to walk out on me, I'll suspend my skepticism and take this a step further. Why are you hoarding all that history?"

"It bothers you that I'm selfishly keeping these cultural gems to myself."

"Doesn't that bother you?"

"No, because that's not what I'm doing."

"Help me out here." Jax propped an elbow on the table. "I'm having a hard time wrapping my head around this. How did you acquire all those rare artifacts? Surely, you don't have that kind of disposable money?"

"None were expensive, monetarily speaking. Most came into my possession because I was in the right place at the right time, I knew the right people, and I was deemed responsible and trustworthy. It's complicated to explain. Think of it as a type of inheritance for historical safe-keeping."

"Then you plan to eventually pass them on to someone."

"You could say that. I'm protecting them for posterity to donate to museums or to sell them at auction to collectors. In the auction scenario, the money will go to charities. I have lesser assets to support my meager needs and expenses when I need them."

"What you're saying without saying it is you're financially well-off."

"Comfortable. Financially comfortable."

"Then why do you move around from job to job? For that matter, why do you work at all? Why don't you travel? See the world."

"I have traveled the world. Many times. Undoubtedly, I'll travel it again. It's not possible for me to stay in one place too long. So I work for a paycheck, same as you."

"That doesn't answer my question."

Lissa's shoulders fell on a slow exhale. "Mostly, I work to keep boredom at bay. I work for the satisfaction of being good at what I do. Working with animals, particularly horses, gives my life purpose. I feel as if I'm contributing something useful to society. As for moving, well, there are certain aspects about me that, over time and familiarity, people become..." She paused, gathered her thoughts. "Let's leave it that I make people uneasy."

Jax looked at her for a long time, slowly shaking his head. "There is a disconcerting mystery about you. I can't put my finger on exactly what, but I'm intrigued."

"We all have secrets."

"Apparently, some more than others. Let's get to firmer footing. What brought you to Colorado?" He was fishing for information, and he didn't doubt for a second that she knew it.

"Wanderlust. Just following the sunset. I wanted to see the Great Plains as they spread out from the foot of the Rocky Mountains. What about you? Are you a native Coloradoan?"

He took her redirection for what it was for and went with it. "I am. Born and raised right here. Other than when I went to college, which was just 60 miles away in Greeley, I've never lived anywhere else. Never wanted to."

"What did you study?"

"Business administration and accounting. To make sure I graduated with a well-rounded educational experience, as my advisor called it, I minored in psychology."

"Psychology? That surprises me. You don't come across as the touchy-feeling sort."

"I'm not, and it surprised everyone else, too. The classes were easy enough, and the subject matter was interesting up to a point."

"What point was that?"

"The point where it became hogwash."

Her laughing giggle brought a rosy tint to her cheeks that accentuated her natural beauty. And, putting her outrageous stories aside, it was easy to talk to her. Jax found himself slipping into conversation about the Granger family's history with horseracing. By the time they ordered the second carafe of after-dinner coffee, only one other couple remained. Jax relaxed, content in the cozy ambience of their corner nook, but when Lissa placed her linen napkin down and pushed back from the table, he had a disheartening feeling the end of their date had arrived.

"Dance with me."

Not what he'd expected. "Here? There's no dance floor or musicians."

"Don't be so limited in your imagination. We have elevator music and a dim corner. That's all we need. Take off your jacket." Standing, she kicked off her heels and motioned for him to come around to her side. Draping his jacket over her chair, she led him away from the table.

A Dean Martin wannabe crooned an old, slow tune as she slipped into his arms. Undoing his tie, Lissa let the ends hang loosely around his neck, then she opened the top three buttons of his shirt. Resting her cheek on his shoulder, she whispered, "Your cologne is heady. Musky, but not sweet or overpowering. I like the way it blends with your other male aromas."

Jax frowned. "You're saying I smell funny?"

With a light giggle, she explained, "No, but there's an elusive suggestion of leather, alfalfa, and horses about you. It's...disturbing."

"Disturbing bad, or disturbing arousing?"

"Definitely arousing."

He hugged her to him, swaying with easy steps. It felt so natural to have her in his arms. Inhaling the fresh scent of her hair, he said, "You usually have a sterile, medicinal aroma, but tonight you smell wonderfully like a woman. Soapy fresh and summery. Feminine and utterly enticing."

What the hell was happening to him? He'd gone from just wanting to get her into bed to never wanting this dance to end. Holding her a little closer, he placed a light kiss on her cheek. Leaning back, she tilted her head to look at him.

"You want to kiss me."

It was a fact he wouldn't deny. "Will you stop me?"

"Yes.

"Why?"

"Because I want you to kiss me with all of the passion I see in your eyes. I want the feeling of your mouth on mine, curling my toes and setting loose butterflies in my stomach. I want the world to stop spinning for those few unforgettable moments of your kiss."

This confession, this glimpse of her feelings for him, touched a place in his heart no woman had ever found, and his heart responded.

"But," she touched his lips with her fingers, "it's not the right time for that kiss. It's too soon." She stepped out of his arms, a soft shine of regret and reluctance in her eyes. "Dinner and talking to you was wonderful, and this dance... Your arms around me... I haven't felt this way in a long time. A very long time." Her voice faded to a rueful whisper. "There are things about me I can't explain yet, and my emotions are moving faster than my desire to control them."

"That means you care for me."

"More than is good for either of us."

He pulled her back into his arms and whispered close to her ear, "Stay with me tonight. My place or yours. Just don't leave me."

She shook her head and kissed him lightly on the lips then backed away. "The temptation is strong. So strong. But not tonight. You're not ready for me, and I'm certainly not ready for you. But I brought you something." From her evening bag, she removed a small cloth drawstring bag that reminded him of the little cotton bags of golden-colored, nugget-sized bubble gum pieces he tied to his belt loops when he was a kid.

"I made a set of runes for you. I chose stones from my collection that I've gathered over the years. I chose each stone with you in mind. Hold them. Roll them out and study them. Invite them into your life. Open your mind and they will speak to you. Listen with your heart, and they won't steer you wrong."

She placed the bag beside his empty wine glass.

"I wrote an explanation of each symbol on a card. You'll find it's straightforward. My runes represent life in its most simplistic state. I call them Elemental Earth Stones. There's also a cloth to roll them on. The cloth represents the world in which you live. You'll understand once you spend time with them." With a little wave of regret, she said, "Thanks for the evening."

Picking up her stilettos, she dangled the heels from her fingertips and walked away barefooted. Once again, she'd left him standing alone watching her leave.

Jax, old boy, he told himself, *if you're not careful, you're going to mess around and let her walk clear out of your life.*

Shorthanded on transport drivers, Jax made several short-hauls to deliver and pick up horses, then Steve made a trip down into Texas. Mac even took a turn out to California, but Jax insisted on going on the road with the east coast route. He didn't mind. He'd driven transport for years before giving up the road to help Steve run the business full-time. He wished he'd asked Lissa to ride along, despite knowing she'd have declined in favor of her work. He couldn't bring himself to call her at the clinic just to say hello, and he didn't dare just stop by for no good reason. The razzing he'd take from Doc Bohlanger was more than his ego could handle.

The miles of windshield time nearly drove him crazy with missing Lissa. He consoled himself remembering every detail of what he considered their nine official dates, plus, he'd finagled seeing her just about every week since they'd met, even though most meet-ups lasted only a few minutes. Still, time and again, she'd turned down his invitations to cook supper for her at his house or treat her to a night out on the town in Denver.

Worse yet, she hadn't invited him to her place, which remained at the heart of his frustration. He didn't know where she lived, and he didn't have her phone number. When he'd badgered her one too many times, she'd warned, "Let it alone, Jax. There's a song about hanging on loosely. You'd be wise to heed that advice."

He thought about following her some night when she left the clinic, but the flat, open land around Overland Crossing didn't lend itself to clandestine detective work. She'd spot him a mile away and no doubt lead him on a wild goose chase just to entertain herself and prove to him she could. He couldn't figure out why she protected her privacy with the tenacity of a bulldog guarding his bones.

So, here he was, alone and nine hundred miles away from home at his first stop in Chicago. It was on to Cleveland next and then to New York, where he waited for a week to get a full load for the run to Pennsylvania. From there, it was back to Cleveland, drop down to Columbus, and swing over to Chicago before he headed for home. Sometimes, he regretted leaving the bag of Earth stones at home. Not that he put any stock in the fortune telling capability of a rock, but having them with him would have been a nice diversion during the long nights in motel rooms.

He was three weeks on the road when Mandy's call came in. "Happy Birthday, Jax."

He grinned. "Thanks. I'd forgotten."

"Where are you?"

"Just left Chicago and I'm headed for Omaha. I'll go to Grand Island from there. Why?"

"Your dad's here for a quick visit. With your birthdays so close, I want to celebrate with supper for you both this weekend. Can you make it home by Saturday evening? Say, six-ish?"

"Should be able to."

"Grandma Sue and Grandpa Kevin are coming."

"Great."

"How's the trip going?"

"No problems. It just seems like I've been gone a year." Jax tried to sound casual. "So... Has Lissa been around?"

"Yesss." She drew the word out. "Twice already just this week."

He heard the grin in her voice.

"Has she... ah... Has she asked about me?"

"You sound smitten, Jaxon Granger. That's not like you."

Annoyed that she was right, and irate that she was rubbing it in, he asked not so politely, "Well, damn it, did she?"

"Yes, she said she'll call and wish you a happy birthday." Mandy spoke around her giggling. "I invited her to supper on Saturday."

Jax's heart alternately soared and fell. He didn't even mind the sing-songy, teasing lilt in her voice. That Lissa was going to call was as exhilarating as the agony of Saturday being a thousand miles and several stops away.

"I'll be there with bells on."

Mandy giggled. "I'd like to see that. See you on Saturday."

Each mile was an eternity traveled in checking and recheck-ing his phone for the reassurance of service. His anticipation for Lissa's call waned as the hours passed without hearing from her. While still a long way from Omaha, he pulled into a truck stop just as his phone rang. His hopes rose in the same instant he cursed the phone's display for only showing Incoming Call and not an identifying number.

"This is Jax. Speak your business."

"I hear you're thirty-seven today."

Lissa.

"Are you there? Jax?"

Clearing his throat, he said, "Yeah. Yeah, I'm here. That's right. Thirty-seven. I'm getting to be an old man."

She laughed. "You don't know what old is. Where are you?"

"I'm at a truck stop between Chicago and Omaha to refuel and grab a bite to eat." He rolled to a stop at a diesel pump and set the brakes. "Are you on call?"

"As a matter of fact, I am. I'm on my way to the clinic now. I'll likely be here the rest of the night."

"Well, if you get a chance, give me a call. I'll be on the road."

"All right. If I can, I will, but don't count on it. Anyway, I hope you've had a nice birthday."

"Thanks. Not much opportunity to celebrate when you're hauling horses from town to town." He didn't want her to hang up, so he grasped for anything to keep her talking.

"Mandy says you're coming to supper on Saturday."

"Yes."

"Good. You'll get to meet my dad."

"Mandy mentioned that."

"You know, calling and wishing me happy birthday makes me think you called on your personal phone instead of your work phone."

Silence. He waited.

"You're right. I did."

She could have lied. He took it as a good sign that she didn't. He grabbed a pen from the glove box and poised the tip over his palm. "So, what's the number?"

More silence.

"Are you still—"

She recited the numbers.

"Got it. Thanks."

"Don't abuse it."

"You don't want me to call you?"

"I didn't say that."

"Lissa?"

"Yes?"

Say it. Just say it. "I wish you were with me. I've missed you."

Again, nothing from her end. He checked the service. Still connected. "Are you there?"

"Yes, I'm here." Hesitation, then, "I've missed you, too, Jax."

"How much?"

"More than is good for me. Don't push your luck."

The light lilting tone in her voice made him smile. He didn't know what giddiness felt like, but he was pretty sure it must be close to how he felt right then.

"Jax, I've reached the clinic. I have to go."

"Yeah, sure. It was good talking to you. See you Saturday."

Leaning back in his seat, he sat there staring at the center of the steering wheel as he worked her words around in his head. She admitted it. She misses me. And it sounded like she wasn't just saying the words. She meant it. His slow grin turned to a full-blown smile.

A full thermos of coffee, an extra sandwich and chips for the road, and the tanks full of diesel, Jax hit the highway. Light-hearted and counting off the miles, he turned up the volume on the classic country music radio station and sang his way homeward on Interstate 80. It was somewhere west of Grand Island when he realized he was in love.

I'll be a son of a bitch.

Chapter Six

An hour after unloading the last of the horses at a thorough-bred horse ranch outside of Denver, Jax was home and backing his rig into place. Grabbing his duffle from the sleeper, he walked toward his house with the single-minded intent of a steaming hot shower, scotch on the rocks, and a nap. As he crossed the yard, Patrick and Steve met him.

"Hey, big brother."

"Hi, Steve."

"Good to see you, Jax. How was the trip?" Patrick slapped Jax on the back.

"Good to see you, too, Dad. The trip was uneventful, inter-minable, but financially profitable. How's Phoenix?"

They walked toward Steve's house.

"Same as always. I'm running twenty to twenty-five head. It's good."

"I'm surprised you're here. The Phoenix season is over in a few weeks. What brings you home this early?"

"I needed some papers from my safety deposit box at the bank. Business. Some routine legal things."

Jax nodded. "We could have sent them to you and saved you the drive."

"I know, but I needed to look through the papers myself. I wasn't sure what I was looking for was even in the box."

"Makes sense. So, how did you get away from Steve's kids? I'm amazed they let you out of their sight."

"Lindsey's napping, and the other two are impatiently waiting for her to wake so they can go gadding around town. I heard something about shopping, ice cream, a matinee, and feeding the ducks at Platte River Park."

Steve interjected, "They'll be back by bedtime."

"Sounds like a big outing."

"It is. They're pretty excited."

Jax's stride slowed. "Mandy said she was cooking supper." This wasn't adding up, and the stolen glance Steve cut toward Patrick confirmed it. "Who's taking them out on the town if Mandy's not going?"

"Helen."

"Aunt Helen is taking three little kids all by herself to the movie, shopping, ducks, and ice cream?"

Patrick nodded, and Steve nodded along with him, stammering, "Uh... well... she's not by herself. Grandma's going along, and they're meeting up with someone else. A friend who's in town for a short visit."

Jax looked between them. "Something's going on here, but I'm too tired to care." When it came down to it, his mother's widowed sister was as close to Steve's kids as Grandma Sue, so this wasn't that unusual for her to dote upon them. "I've gotta get a couple hours of sleep. I'll be over around six."

Once inside his house, Jax kicked his boots off, poured two inches of scotch over ice, and went to his bedroom. He stood at his dresser where he'd left the drawstring bag of runes. Not that he put any credence into fortune telling, he had messed with them enough to get a feel for how they worked. Grudgingly, he admitted to an interest of sorts with how the rune-rocks connected with one another when he rolled them out, and that there was some relationship to aspects of his life. Still, how could rocks with pictures drawn on them hold real information about his life, or anyone else's for that matter?

His attention moved to his drawings of the recurring dream, which he'd slipped into the wooden border of the dresser's mirror. He supposed fortune-telling cards were no sillier than dream interpretation. Finishing off the scotch, he stripped down on his way to the shower with the realization that his dream hadn't returned since he'd met Lissa.

Jax spied Lissa's vet truck parked between Dave Bohlanger's truck and his grandparent's car as he crossed the yard to Steve's house. His steps quickened. Damn, but it had been a long time since he'd seen Lissa. Mandy met him at the door with a hug and rubbed her fingers along his jaw. "What's this? Growing your beard out again? The mustache is a nice touch. I like it. Supper's in the slow cooker, and I'm just about done with the salad. It's a nice evening. We'll eat out on the deck."

"My favorite?"

"Of course. Beef and noodles with homemade bread."

"Chocolate pudding cake for dessert?"

"Would I make any other kind of dessert for you and Patrick? You're both chocolate fiends."

He pecked a kiss on her cheek. "Can't beat that with a stick."

Dave and Judy Bohlanger, sitting at the kitchen table, wished him a happy birthday, as did his grandparents. Steve handed him a beer on his meandering way toward the living room in search of Lissa. He found her sitting beside his dad on the couch. When she looked up, Jax caught an unguarded gleam of I missed you shining in her eyes that she hastily covered with a sip from her glass of iced tea. Maybe it meant the night held a promise of something intimate between them.

Resisting the urge to walk right over and kiss her, Jax tipped his beer instead. "I'm glad you came by tonight."

She smiled. "How can I say no to Mandy? She's a jewel."

"She certainly is."

Mac greeted him, "Happy Birthday, old boy. Have a good trip?"

"Thanks, and I did, but I hope we find a driver soon. I don't travel as well as I used to."

"I hear what you're saying," Mac agreed. "We had two fellas inquire while you were gone. One has potential. I'll fill you in later."

"Sounds good."

Lissa gave Jax a long, narrow package wrapped in birthday paper.

Jax turned it over then shook it. "*Hmm*. It rattles. Can I open it now?"

"Yes."

He tore off the paper and a grin spread across his face. "Candy in the shape of horseshoes. I do love dark chocolate." Looking at Lissa, he said, "Thank you."

"You're welcome. Each piece is filled with bourbon."

"Ah... I see that now. Double thanks."

Mac peered over Jax's shoulder. "You gonna keep it all to yourself?"

Chucking, Jax gave the box to Mac. "Help yourself, and pass it around."

"Jax," Patrick interjected, "Lissa and I have been talking. I've encouraged her to come to Phoenix if things don't pan out here. There's always work for good vets on the track."

Jax didn't like that. He didn't like the idea of Lissa going so far away unless he went with her, and he had no plans to leave. He started to say something to that effect just when Mandy called them to supper. The group convened outside on the deck. The meal and conversation passed amiably, and though he was impatient to be alone with Lissa there was no getting away from Mandy's supper celebration this early. He didn't really mind. It was good to sit and visit with family and friends. He hadn't done that in a long time.

Jax saw Mandy check her watch then exchange glances with Steve and Patrick, who gave her an imperceptible nod.

"Okay, everyone. I have a special birthday surprise for Jax. Grab your drinks and follow me into the office."

Jax looked around the group then at Mandy, his grin widening. "A cake and a stripper with big—"

"Keep it clean," Mandy cautioned as she tugged him by the hand.

"Then what is it?"

"A peek into your future." Indicating one of the two chairs in front of the computer, she said, "Take a seat, Birthday Boy. The rest of you gather around so you can see the screen." She sat in the other chair, gave the mouse a jiggle. "This is a brand new, cutting-edge website on the Internet. I discovered it at the first of the year." A neon pink background filled the screen with the words *Tarot Readings—Let the Cards Guide Your Future* emblazoned across the center.

Jax grimaced then cut a suspicious look at Lissa. "Do you know about this?"

She shook her head. "Nope. Not a thing."

He shot a glare at Steve, who pointed at Mandy. "Blame her. She concocted this idea. I'm just here for the beer and fireworks when you find out what's really going on."

Jax bristled at Steve's evasive taunt, which was well-honed torment as only his little brother could produce.

Mandy shushed Steve with a glower that warned he'd said too much.

"So, what the hell's really going on?"

Mandy flinched when he jabbed her in the ribs. Batting his hand away, she said, "Patience, young grasshopper."

Patrick held a fresh beer in front of Jax. "Here. I put a shot of tequila in it. Slam it. You're going to need it, and a few more, before this night's over."

"What—"

"Be quiet, drink your beer, and pay attention," Mandy redirected him. "Now, just follow the instructions."

"Where did you come up with this hair-brained idea?"

Mandy made a face. "It's not hair-brained, and it's your own fault. While you were on the road, I gathered your laundry to send it out to your service, since you weren't here to take it yourself. I came across a most intriguing drawstring bag on your dresser. You can imagine my surprise to discover the rune stones inside. I've never come across anything even remotely similar. They're a wonderfully simplistic rendition of runes that capture the pagan beliefs of the interconnectedness of the five elements. Where did you get them?"

He blew out a slow sigh. *What was the line? For 'tis the sport to have the engineer hoisted with his own petard. Something like that.*

He caught himself sending an accusing glance toward Lissa, then shrugged, and tried to sound disinterested. "A friend left them. What does it matter? You know I don't believe in this."

Mandy raised her eyebrows. "If you don't believe in it, why did you leave them in plain sight?"

He had no comeback, just a go-to-hell look that made her all the more satisfied in her righteousness.

"That's what I thought. You can't play innocent with me, Jaxon Granger. You've been hiding a mystic side. That' why I decided you should do a tarot reading tonight. Now, follow the instructions on the screen. It's all set up. Here, I'll get you started. Concentrate on this question: What is essential for me to know right now in my life? Then point and click—"

"I can read." His sharp tone masked his discomfort. He took a long pull on his beer before clicking the mouse four times on the virtual tarot deck. Four cards that meant nothing to him appeared face up and side-by-side. Mumbling, he read, "This is a modified four-card Karmic Spread. Whatever the hell that is."

Steve goaded him, "Karma, huh? Now we'll all find out what kind of life you've really been living."

Jax leaned back. "My karma is just fine the way it is. So, I'll say it again. This is bull—"

Mandy wagged her index finger in his face. "Don't be so judgmental just because you don't understand it. There are influences in our lives that none of us understands, and I believe tarot cards are one way to gain a glimpse into those mysteries. Never take the cards lightly." She tapped the screen. "Look here. In this spread, you are the seeker of your karmic lessons."

Jax took another swig of beer and willingly conceded the moment to Mandy.

"The purpose is to help you sort out why you continue to repeat certain behaviors and hold on to emotional baggage that keeps you from moving to the next phase of your life."

"In other words, this spread will show my level of insanity."

"Insanity?"

"Yeah, Einstein said doing the same thing over and over the same way and expecting different results each time defines insanity."

"Oh, no, it's not insanity at all. It's all about the spiritual and emotional journey that you must take in order to reach your destiny."

Jax shook his head. For all her out-there beliefs, Mandy was painfully literal in her thinking at times. Like now.

Drumming her fingertips on the edge of the table, Mandy admonished, "Jaxon Patrick Granger, pay attention."

"All right, all right. I'm reading. I'm reading." Jax skimmed, mumbling the highlights. "More positive than negative energy. Wheel of Fortune always means fate greeting in a positive way. Reminder that the time is now to attend to destiny. Turning point in your life. Begin to experience great change. Card reversed—"

Mandy took charge. "We'll be here all night at your snail's pace. Let me interpret. The Wheel of Fortune reversed indicates a lack of momentum in your life right now. You're stagnating in your same old habits, which are getting you nowhere. You have to regain control of where your life is going, because the wheel of your life is on an uphill turn right now. If you want influence over the outcome, begin an honest internal dialogue with yourself. You'll start to recognize patterns of behavior that have outlived their usefulness, so you need to prepare yourself for a powerful epiphany in the near future. It will be life-altering."

Jax shifted in his chair and cast a glance at Lissa. "Life-altering. Not sure I like the sound of that."

Mandy tapped his arm. "There's more. The Two of Cups indicates the union of two people along with the emotional connections involved in a relationship. This card emphasizes the power of love and friendship that can heal wounds of the heart. The keyword here is symbiosis. This card always means the arrival of a new partner in a potentially loving and romantic relationship, whether upright or reversed. However, see the sentinel watching over the couple?" She touched her fingertip to the screen. "It represents a higher authority that influences the joining of that couple. Upright, it symbolizes all that is good in a relationship, but this one is reversed. That means the sentinel is distant from the couple, not as powerful for positive outcomes, which can mean disharmony of major proportions for them."

"It doesn't take a tarot card to tell me I'm not good with long-term relationships." Peripherally, he saw Lissa gazing, eyes downcast, at a point on the floor.

"Well, the good part of this is you have the opportunity to internalize the futility of your old habits and make positive changes. A new relationship can be successful if stubbornness doesn't impede communication. A point of caution with the Two of Cups reversed is that emotions run completely wild if given free rein. Moderation and self-awareness are critical."

"You really believe this, don't you?"

Nodding enthusiastically, Mandy said, "Now, look at this. The last two cards are both upright, which is very encouraging."

"What?" Jax looked at the screen then at Mandy. "One's called Judgment, and the other is Death. How the hell is that encouraging?"

"Jax, the Death card rarely suggests actual death."

"Death is death. It's as final as final can be." Jax tilted his beer bottle toward her to make his point.

"Not necessarily. One must interpret this card as symbolic death, as in the closure of something old for the inevitable something new arriving to replace it." Mandy tapped the screen again. "See what it says here. Your life has been full of frivolous excesses and disregard for what's truly important. You've led a superficial life, and it's time to cut yourself free from that so you can be reborn—figuratively, of course."

"A born-again non-believer?" Jax's patience with this birthday present was growing thin.

"Very funny. Ha-ha. No, it indicates radical change and a turning point in your life. Think of it as a consequence of your past behaviors and attitudes. Transformation is its key descriptor." Sitting back in her chair, Mandy nodded while looking at the computer screen. "Jax, there are inexorable forces at work here. This is a powerful layout."

Steve leaned over Jax's shoulder to peer at the screen. "So, the Judgment card signifies your awakening and your life moving into a new cycle. It says it's a rite of passage that brings a paradigm shift."

"Paradigm shift. Now that's a trite and used-up cliché." Jax gulped a swallow of beer.

Mandy bumped his foot with hers. "Then think of it as your cosmic wake-up call. The end of your present world as you know it. Discovering a higher purpose in life beyond your self-centeredness. It represents redemption for your past transgressions with the opportunity for atonement toward those you've hurt. It's about revelations and letting go of value judgments. Forgive and be forgiven."

"Great. I feel like I'm back in Sunday school."

"Quit complaining. We're nearly finished. Now, click on the 'More' arrow for the overall summary and closure. All right. Here we go. It says: The number two is woven throughout the cards. Two means balance, relationship, and intuition. The reversed cards are a reminder to pay particular attention to their messages, as you need to learn to handle relationships better. These are your karmic lessons. The three Major Arcana cards—'"

"Major what cards?"

"Arcana. Just listen. Where was I? Oh...here. With three of the four cards you chose being Major Arcana, what is happening in your life now is fated to happen whether you work with it or not. Events are already in motion, and you can't change them. It is your destiny, and it is out of your hands."

"That sounds like giving up my free will."

"The line between free will and destiny is a blurry one, for sure. However, you have control of the choices that are yet to manifest as you reach your destiny. You can influence the outcome of your life if you truly pay attention to the messages in this reading. You can learn from the past behaviors that have gotten you nowhere." Mandy looked at him. "I'm not an expert reader by any means, but I do know the Wheel of Fortune reversed also warns to pay special attention to a chance encounter. It will change your life whether you want it to or not."

He admitted the chance encounter with Lissa had already changed his life, and it made him uncomfortable that he couldn't offhandedly dismiss everything in this reading as it related to his life. However, he still wasn't about to give it serious credence.

Mandy hit the print button. "Even as a dyed-in-the-wool skeptic, you have to admit there's some truth in the cards."

"Nope. I won't admit anything. It's the Forer Effect. Plain and simple."

"It most certainly is not," Mandy countered.

"What's the Forer Effect?" Steve asked.

Lissa spoke before Jax or Mandy had a chance. "It's also called the Barnum Effect. It's a psychological situation in which people accept what they think is a tailored description of their personality when, in actuality, the description is generally vague and applicable to just about anyone. Another term for it is acceptance phenomenon."

"Got it. Like horoscopes."

"Exactly like horoscopes," Jax agreed.

Mandy handed him the printout. "Regardless, here's a keepsake." Looking at the clock, she said, "Well, the kids should be home any minute. I'm going to start their bath. Help yourself to drinks, and there's still dessert left."

The Bohlangers said their goodnights. The others followed Mandy out of the room. Once they were alone, Jax swiveled his chair to look at Lissa.

"You believe all of this, don't you?"

She nodded. "I do. I've seen enough to know there are mysteries at work in our lives. We have to take them on faith, as they're unavoidable and, ultimately, for our own good."

"Faith? Like religion?"

"Not at all. Religion is too limiting in the larger spiritual perspective. There are outside influences that mold our lives in ways we can't see or even imagine. We can question, and we have free will to choose, but we can't ignore the power of fate and destiny."

Standing, he drew her to him and wrapped his arms around her waist. "I need to talk to you. Serious talk. Stay with me tonight."

"I have some things to say to you, especially after that tarot reading. Jax, that reading also spoke to my life."

"Then will you? Stay with me?"

The kitchen door opened, and the ensuing ruckus of happy children noises and Mandy's voice rising over the din with instructions to head toward the bathtub effectively interrupted Lissa's response.

"Come on, Grandma Linda," Marci said.

"I'll be along in a minute, sweetie."

Jax spun around, stumbling over Lissa's feet. He locked his gaze on the doorway, listening, not believing what he'd heard. He stood rooted to the floor in stunned shock. How long had it been since he'd heard her voice? He walked into the kitchen and greeted her.

"What the hell are you doing here?"

"Well, hello, yourself, Jax. It's nice to see you. I'm sorry you're disappointed that I'm here. I mean that. I'm truly sorry...about so many things."

Jax couldn't deal with the sincere warmth in her words. His anger spiked, and he dropped a hard glare on Steve. "Just a friend in town for a short visit, huh? Obviously, this little soiree is more than a birthday celebration."

Patrick intervened. "That's right. We need to have a family talk, and it can't wait any longer. We knew if we told you the truth, you wouldn't come here tonight."

He looked at his dad. "Thanks for the swell birthday present. So, what's going on? I told you last time we all got together for a little family pow-wow that I was finished talking."

"Things have changed—"

Jax's temper, fueled by years of hurt and feelings of abandonment, exploded. "Nothing's changed!" He leveled a black gaze at his mother. "You walked out on us for a career. You left your husband and two kids, so you could run off and work in a man's world. So, suck it up, Buttercup, and take it like a man. I told you the only sympathy you'll get from me is in the dictionary. You'll find it right between shit and syphilis."

Unmoved, Patrick went on, "For years we've all tried to explain what happened, but you've never listened. You never once listened when we wanted to tell you the circumstances of our divorce—"

"What's there to understand?" Jax turned on his mother. "One day we were a family, and the next you'd left grad school with a shiny new degree and a job in Africa. After that, you showed up just often enough to clear your conscience and rip my guts out when you left. Do you have any idea what that did to me as a kid?"

Steve stepped up. "Jax, in Mom's defense, I kept in touch with her all along. She hasn't been in Africa for years. If you weren't so damned pigheaded, you'd have known that. We stopped keeping you in the loop, because you always went into tirades when we mentioned her."

Jax's laugh wasn't pleasant. "You know, I don't really give a flying f—"

"Your mother and I remarried New Year's Day. New year. New beginning." Patrick lifted Linda's left hand for Jax to see her wedding band.

Jax stared at them, realization taking shape. Turning to Steve, he said, "So that's the real reason you and Mandy took the kids to Phoenix for the Christmas holiday."

Steve nodded. "Yeah. It is. Jax. It's so bad with you that we bribed the kids not to say anything about spending time with their grandma. And let me tell you, it's not easy to get little kids to be quiet."

Peripherally, Jax saw Lissa slipping around behind him and heading toward the patio door. "Lissa, wait." He brushed past his mother and caught Lissa's hand. "Don't. Don't go."

"This is private family talk. I'm an outsider. I don't belong here."

"You're wrong. You're not an outsider. Not with me." He'd never needed a woman before, only wanted, but the words came easily now. For the first time in his life, he said words to a woman that came from his heart. "I need you to stay. With me. Here. Now."

She shook her head. "Maybe you should take what the cards told you as a sign, and face whatever issues are festering inside your heart so you can move on. It's called seeking closure. Until you do, you'll never be able to accept what's in my past and what that means in my life now, or what it will mean in yours."

Looking past Jax, Lissa said, "Steve, give Mandy my thanks for a wonderful supper." Then she nodded to Patrick and Linda. "It was nice to meet you."

Patrick said, "We'll talk later about my offer to come to Phoenix."

Lissa only nodded.

Mac followed her lead. "Time for me to head home, too. Lissa, I'll walk you out. Thanks, Steve, for the grub and drinks."

Once again, Jax watched Lissa leave with the reluctant realization that it was time to fish or cut bait, as his Grandpa Kevin liked to say. But, if staying here and dealing with the shadows of his past was what it took not to lose Lissa, then he'd see it through. With a deep breath and a hard exhale, he set his shoulders and turned to face his parents and Steve.

"All right, I'm listening."

Chapter Seven

Jax brought his pickup to a rolling stop in front of Lissa's old farmhouse. He wasn't surprised she didn't have a yard light, and he didn't need one since the coming full moon illuminated the surroundings enough to see the dilapidated outbuildings, the falling-down corral, and the barn that strangely resembled the one in his dream. That realization sent goosebumps scuttling along his arms. He'd known about this place all his life, even visited it a few times as a youngster when his dad hauled horses here to use the only training track within a hundred miles, but the place, like many early childhood memories, had faded over the years. Now he recalled that when the old fellow who'd owned it died without heirs, the place had gone into disrepair and disregard. Some years later, the land was purchased by a neighbor with adjoining land, and they'd fixed up the house to rent to people who liked solitude in a simple setting. Somehow, this place fit Lissa.

The sound of gravel crunching under his boots on his way to the front door seemed unnaturally loud in the still, silent night. Lissa opened the door before he knocked. Silhouetted by the muted amber glow of candlelight, her long gauzy skirt caught a light breeze and fluttered around her legs.

"You're not surprised to see me."

"That's right."

"Why didn't you answer my calls?"

"I didn't want to."

"Why not?"

"You have so much anger and hurt penned up inside you, that releasing it is not a talk-on-the-phone situation, especially not with me. You need to talk to your family. That's where it has to be worked out."

"We talked, and we found common ground to build on. It's shaky ground, but it's a place to start. Do you want to know?"

"Only if it's important for you to tell me."

"It is."

"Then I'm listening."

He looked around. "Can we talk someplace other than your doorway?"

"Let's walk."

They were nearly to the end of the quarter-mile driveway before Jax spoke. "I've badgered Doc Bohlanger to tell me where you live since the day after we met. When you didn't answer my calls tonight, he finally caved and told me. It must have been my desperate begging that got to him."

"No. I called him when I left your place and told him to tell you, but to make you work for it."

Jax shook his head, chagrined. "You could have told me yourself."

"Where's the satisfaction in that?"

He cocked his head and studied her. "I can't tell if you're teasing or slapping my fingers."

"A little of both, I suppose. Jax, you're much too used to getting what you want just because you're Jaxon Granger and you think you deserve it. You've needed a good dose of humble in your life. I was just doing my part tonight to help you catch up on your quota."

"All right. I deserved that." They walked on a few steps in silence. "Humble. Now there's a word. I've been hit right between the eyes with a big, fat humble stick tonight."

"How so?"

They started back toward the house.

"I've hated my mother since I was fifteen years old. I hated that she left us. I hated that she broke my dad's heart. I hated—" He blew out a hard breath to get a handle on the memories and the feelings that went with them. "Apparently, love was the cause of my parents' divorce."

"That's an interesting quandary."

"You have no idea. On the drive here, I relived the years I've wasted in self-pity and self-righteous judgment. I used them as an emotional crutch, excuses to take my anger out on all women who got too close to me. I see now that once any woman gave me her heart, that I had no more use for them. I also see how I threw their feelings back at them, just like I was convinced my mom had done to me. All love meant to me was betrayal and lies, and I had to be quicker on the betrayal draw to keep my barricade of righteousness from crumbling."

"That must have been quite a talk to have brought about this depth of insight."

Jax kicked a stone and watched it skip along the path ahead of them. "Believe it or not, those damn tarot cards had something to do with it. It all started to fall into place and make sense. All I had to do was listen to what people had been trying to get through my thick skull all these years. I just wouldn't listen or believe them."

"Sometimes, the truth is right there in front of us, but we can't see it because our emotions work as blinders to block what we don't want to face—or accept."

Jax nodded. "Yeah. Blinders is a good descriptor. My mother sank into a crippling depression not long after Steve was born. Nothing worked to pull her out of it. Dad tried everything he could think of. Finally, he convinced her to enroll in college to get her focused on something outside of herself. It seemed to work. She started coming out of it, and life went along okay for a while—at least, on the surface.

"But even with the upswing in her mental health, their marriage was in trouble by then. When she graduated with her degree in cultural anthropology, a career opportunity in Africa came along that she couldn't pass up."

"This was all new to you tonight?"

"Some of it." He removed his hat and ran his fingers through his hair. "Hell, I was a kid, and not sensitive to anything but myself. I knew she was unhappy, but I didn't know the extent. They tried to explain, but I wasn't listening. They eventually stopped trying. I do remember my folks having a big fight over her taking the job in Africa. I got in the middle of it and accused her of hating us. I told her she was a lousy mother for putting her needs ahead of ours, and that a real mother would love us more than that and be home more often." He put his hat back on. "Along with a lot of other fifteen-year-old bullshit. I told her I wouldn't miss her when she was gone."

"That's not uncommon between parents and teenagers."

"But I took that disagreeable teenager-ness to a level that was downright mean. I found out tonight the real sacrifice came from my dad."

"It's also not unusual for kids to be oblivious to what their parents are dealing with. Parents tend to protect their children from adult problems."

Jax nodded, thinking about just how right she was. "I remember that about a week after the argument they'd had over her move to Africa, Dad changed his mind and insisted she leave. His anger was gone. He was nervous, and he didn't let her out of his sight for even a minute until he drove her to the airport and saw her get on the plane." Jax cut a glance toward Lissa. "Let me tell you, I was one confused kid. All I knew was she was going to another continent to work, and my dad, my solid, down-to-earth dad, was a basket case to the point he broke down and cried. That was it for me. That was the moment I hated her."

"And tonight, they told you what really happened."

"Yeah. A couple of days after that big fight, Dad happened to come home early before Steve and I got off the bus, and he'd found Mom unconscious in the bedroom. She'd tried to kill herself. He and my grandparents hid that from us. We knew something terrible had happened, because she was in the hospital. We just didn't know what it was. They said she'd had an accident, and she'd be okay, but we couldn't see her. She had to have complete rest. When she came home, she was...different. I know now she was drugged-up on anti-depressants. About three weeks later, she left for Africa. She seemed glad to be rid of us in an apathetic, tired sort of way. I know now she wasn't glad. She was too medicated for her real emotions to show through."

"Depression is a black, life-sucking hole. Once you've been there, it's difficult not to return."

"I'm beginning to understand that. You know, looking back, I recall lying in bed at night and hearing her crying. It was a heavy burden my father shouldered to shelter Steve and me from her mental illness." He balled up his fist and pressed it against his belly. "It gives me a sick, empty feeling of regret. I was so wrapped up in myself I didn't see what was happening. I should have been a support for my dad and Steve. As it was, Steve took it on himself to be Dad's rock, when he was way too young to be that strong."

"Now that you know, can you make peace with the past? Can you forgive yourself and your parents, particularly your mother?"

"I don't know. Yes. Maybe. The key is forgiving myself. I don't know if I can do that." He shook his head on a hard exhale. "I've caused a lot of heartache for a lot of people, when they were dealing with their own troubles. Funny thing, though. They never stopped trying to reach me despite how I treated them."

"It's called unconditional love."

He nudged another rock with the toe of his boot and sent it skittering and bouncing. "One thing's for sure, I've transferred a lot of misdirected emotion over the last twenty-some years by hating a woman my dad sent away in order to save her life." He looked at Lissa. "There's a nasty bit of irony in that."

She entwined her fingers with his. "Life is full of bitter, horrible ironies."

"What does that mean?"

Their joined hands swung gently. "It means that I have regrets in my life, too."

"Like what?"

"Not long before my husband died, I made a life and death decision."

"You said you decided to live. And I'm glad you did." He squeezed her hand.

Lissa stopped at the back of his pickup. "You may not still feel that way when I explain some things about me."

Jax put down the tailgate and gave her a boost up to sit on it. She arranged her skirt, crossed her ankles, and gently swung her legs.

"Try me. I've been perfecting my listening skills tonight."

He took her hand and brought it to his lips to press a kiss against her knuckles. She touched his cheek with her index finger, ran it over his lips, then traced over his chin and down his neck where she lingered, absently caressing his carotid artery.

He put his hands on her knees with gentle pressure to test her reception to accepting him closer to her. She didn't resist, so he spread her legs and moved in between her thighs. He slid his hands up and down her bare arms.

"Your skin is cool. Do you need a jacket?"

"No. I hardly notice. I have an unusual metabolism. I stay perpetually cool."

"I know how to warm you up." His hands wandered to her hips, then he rolled his palms along her thighs, caressing, and gently gathering and tugging handfuls of her skirt to expose her bare legs.

She stopped his exploration. "Jax. For us to go forward, I have to tell you more about who I am."

"All right."

"And you have to accept what you hear."

"I'm listening."

"Listening isn't the same as hearing."

"I've learned to do both tonight. I promise. Go on."

Lissa stared past him and into the darkness beyond the driveway. She raised her gaze to the cloudless sky. "The stars are so clear and stark against the sky. I enjoy the solitude. The secrecy. The safety."

"So, you're acquainted with the night."

She smiled, nodded. "I like that poem. Yes, I am acquainted with the night. We're close friends, the night and I. So many years I've looked at these stars...the moon. They're my link to the past. My point of grounding when I lose my way. My connection to who I was, who I am now, and who I'll be tomorrow. They've been loyal and constant companions when there was no one else in my life. The moon and stars are the only things I can count on never changing."

Dropping her gaze to look at Jax, she said, "I've worked in some aspect of veterinary medicine since I first volunteered in London with the Royal Army Veterinary Corps."

"I thought I detected a hint of an accent in some of your words. So, you were in the military."

"The year was 1796."

"What—" Jax leaned back, his mind struggling for words. "Well... That was a long time ago." He tilted his head as he eyed her. Skepticism overrode his agreement to hear what she had to say while doing his damnedest to keep an open mind and not laugh outright.

"Yes, it was. King George III was on the throne of England. It was the year Catherine the Great and Robert Burns died. John Adams carried the electoral and popular votes over Thomas Jefferson to become the second U. S. President."

"What have you been doing all the years since?" There was no masking the flippancy in his voice.

"I spent the eighteenth century in Europe wandering, experiencing. Learning. Figuring out how to come to terms with my life, such as it was. I grieved the loss of loved ones and friends along with the destruction of my hopes and dreams. On recommendations and the influence of friends in well-placed positions, along with my knowledge of horses, I was accepted into a veterinary school in London despite being female. I dressed as a man, and only a few of the higher-ups knew the truth. Money changed hands, and the college gained a substantial endowment when I graduated with honors. Later, I earned another medical degree in Norway, and then I moved to Canada. I stayed in the northern areas to take advantage of the longer nights and lesser amounts of direct sunlight—"

"Because of your sensitivity."

"Yes, but that's simplistic. Bear with me. When England entered World War I, I returned to London for the duration of the war, and then I joined the U.S. Veterinary Corps and came to America in 1921."

"And I rode with Custer." He snorted a laugh. "You spin a great yarn. Even better than the one you told about your vault full of treasures."

Her eyes narrowed and darkened.

His smile faded. "You really expect me to believe you."

"I have no reason to fabricate stories. There is more to the *treasures*, as you call them. I'm one of seven individuals dedicated to acquiring and preserving historic artifacts. Why and how aren't important, but I'll tell you I'm responsible for the safe-keeping of the artifacts in my possession, and I have taken a blood oath to protect them. Wine collecting is my own diversion."

Shaking his head, Jax took hold of her shoulders in a compassionate gesture to bring her back from the delusional world in her mind. "Lissa, this is outlandish, impossible. You need—"

"Stop!" She pushed him away, her eyes flashing with impatience and her anger tight around her eyes. "You are in no position to judge or doubt me. You may think you've suddenly learned to listen, but you haven't."

The threat in her tone got through his thick head how serious she was, but it didn't change his conviction that she needed help. "I am listening, but how can you expect me to believe this? I think you've had a psychotic break sometime in your life, and your mind hasn't recovered. It's okay. There are people who can help you. Psychiatrists."

She fixed him with a dark, intense gaze.

"I was born in London in 1625. When my parents died, I inherited their livery and blacksmith business. I continued to operate it with much success. I married a merchant sailor, and I lived an uneventful, happy life for many years. Then our only child—my darling Juliet— died in the early winter of 1665 during the last plague that hit London. Just a few months later, on September 2nd, 1666 to be exact, the Great Fire ravaged London."

Jax moved from skepticism to concerned compassion for the extreme condition of her mental instability. It was some moments before she spoke, and he held his tongue to see where her delusional mind would take her.

"I died in that fire."

"What do you mean, you *died*?" A skin-prickling shiver coursed along his spine.

"I was releasing horses from my livery to give them a chance to escape the coming firestorm. I saved the horses, but I paid the price with my life when a change in the wind trapped me inside the burning stable." She took a deep breath that she exhaled with a shudder, almost a sob. "It's still so clear in my mind. The night blazed bright as day. The fire roared over the city."

Her trance-like stare drew Jax into her memories. He couldn't break away from the scene developing in his head.

"Flames swallowed me. The heat...the heat was... My skin melted like butter sizzling in a hot skillet. My hair and my clothes burned." She waved at something invisible. "No air. Thick, suffocating smoke. I couldn't see. But I could scream, and I could crawl."

Somehow, in his mind's eye, Jax saw it in a flash of stark clarity as if he were there. For a few terrible seconds, he was trapped in her distant memories. He felt what she felt, heard what she heard, saw what she saw. Too horrible to endure, he wrenched his mind free of those shared images, but she didn't return with him.

Chapter Eight

Lissa clawed the air, grasped for help from an invisible source. Her face contorted in remembered anguish and horror. Tears wetted her cheeks. Her pain was too much to watch. He captured her fingers with his and brought her hands to his chest, holding her tightly to offer his comfort, his protection.

"Hey. Come back from there. It's over. You're okay now. You're not alone."

Her eyes, unfocused and distant, looked through him. Her chest heaved with ragged pants of sobbing terror. Jax took her face between his hands and made her look at him.

"Lissa. You're safe. You're safe." He nodded and offered a little smile of encouragement.

She stared at his face many seconds before coherency returned to her eyes.

"I don't know how, but I saw what happened to you. Well, imagined it. You must have some sort of supernatural mental power or hypnotic influence over me."

"No. If you saw it, then it's you who has the mental power."

Jax wiped her tears. "I'm having a hard enough time sticking with this without you dragging me into your alternate reality."

"You promised you'd listen."

Jax nodded as he blew out a slow breath. "You're right. I did. I'm listening. How were you saved?"

"Lord Burton, a nobleman I'd known since childhood, found me clawing my way along the ground moments before the building collapsed, and he dragged me out of the way. I wanted to live to see my husband again. I begged Lord Burton to help me, to get me to a doctor. He said I was beyond a doctor's skill, but he knew a way to save me."

"I don't understand. Medical care has come a long way since 1666, but if a doctor couldn't help you, what could this Lord Burton do?"

"He could give me another life."

"Another life? I don't follow."

"Long life. Not quite immortality, but centuries of living with extremely slow aging. A shadowy presence in the human world. Living, but not alive. A memory that lingers, but leaves no emotional connection with the people we meet or love and, ultimately, leave. Déjà vu. A dream. Dead, but not."

"Hold it." Caught up as he was in her delusion, it took him a few seconds to shake it off and return to reality. "Dead, but not dead. Undead. As in vampire undead?"

"Yes."

"You expect me to believe you're a vampire?" Delusions were one thing. That she believed she was a vampire took her mental instability to a place he wasn't willing to go.

"I do."

It was a struggle to keep the disdainful sarcasm out of his voice. He didn't succeed. "That's...incredible bordering on ludicrous. But, I'll bite." He suppressed a grin at his pun. "How does something like that happen?"

"It wasn't something he could do without my consent. I had to want it, and I had to say the words."

"What words?"

"*Give me tomorrow*. The details of what he did aren't important. Suffice it to say, he turned me right there in the midst of a blazing inferno. I died so I could live."

"Okay. We're far enough into this tale, which would make a great movie, by the way, that I'll continue to suspend disbelief for the sake of hearing how it ends. After Lord Burton turned you into a vampire, what then? Where did you go? How did you survive all these years?"

"He took me to his estate, which is a refuge, a sanctuary, for our kind. I stayed there for many years while I healed and learned to care about living again. He was a father to me when I had no one else. He's a kind and benevolent man."

"Are there a lot of these places? These vampire sanctuaries?"

"Yes. All over the world. Without them, we couldn't continue to exist. We're actually quite small in number, which makes it easy to move among humans."

"My pragmatic mind says there are logistics about this that don't work."

"Such as?"

"Well, identification, for one. How do you handle that? You have to have some sort of birth and death certificates in order to function in society. You know...taxes, bank account, driver's license, social security. That sort of thing. You'd have to reinvent yourself every eighty or ninety years. Take a different name. Create a new identity."

"We have methods for addressing all of those. It's part of the sanctuary system."

"Don't take this wrong, but you look pretty good for someone born in 1625."

Lissa smiled. "The change from human to vampire alters blood chemistry and body metabolism. My organs work differently than yours. I age at a slower rate than a human."

"Evidently." He returned her smile on a chuckle. "So, you spent some time at this nobleman's estate. How did you explain that to your husband?"

"There's the awful irony. He'd gone down with his ship off the coast of Ireland in a storm the week before the fire. I didn't know of his death until many months later."

Another insight hit him. "The song— 'The Fair Sailor Lad'. It tells his story. Now, it makes a whole lot more sense why you're partial to it."

"Careful. You're letting your sensitive side show through."

"I've had a crash course in sensitivity tonight. Apparently, I'm a fast learner—a *reluctant* fast learner—but I'm doing my damnedest to keep my mind open."

"I understand your struggle to believe me. I've walked in your shoes."

"Would you have made a different decision had you known your husband was dead?"

"Yes. I loved him. He's the only man I've ever loved. When I learned he'd drowned, I wanted to die. I tried to— Don't give me that look. I know what you're thinking."

"How can you die? You said vampires are dead, but not dead. Alive, but not alive. That makes you a weird sort of Schrödinger's cat caught in a state of perpetual life/death limbo."

"That's a perfect analogy. However, vampires can cease to exist. There are ways. Lord Burton, and others, watched over me until my will to exist became stronger than my desire not to exist."

Jax squinted one eye. The apologetic grimace of doubt accentuated his shrug. "You have to admit this is a pretty convoluted story."

"It's true, nonetheless. Every word."

"All right. If it's true, where did vampires come from?"

"What do you mean?"

"What's your creation story? Every culture has one, and I'm not talking about Bram Stoker's story."

"There is a wealth of origin stories. Most are regional tales. Some are more gruesome than others. But they all stem from a peoples' need to make sense of their world, their environment and experiences."

"You're saying no one knows."

"There is truth in all myths and legends, however obscure and hidden that truth may be."

"Reminds me of a line from an old western movie—when the legend becomes fact, go with the legend."

Lissa smiled. "Something like that, yes."

"So what's your favorite legend?"

"It's from Greek mythology. You can pick up any decent collection of mythology and find it there, although it's not one of the better-known stories."

Jax waited, eyebrows raised. "Well? What's the story?"

"Not now."

"Why not?"

"Because you're a skeptic, and I won't waste my breath telling you the story only to have you deride it. You're not ready to hear it, let alone appreciate it."

"Well, you're right. I am skeptical. But, I will concede there was something powerful going on when you talked about the fire. I saw it in my mind as if I was there with you. It's like you can get into my head. You did it that first night we met, like some psychic mental manipulation, if you believe that nonsense, and I don't."

"But can you acknowledge the possibility that what I've said is true?"

"Honestly?" He rubbed his knuckles against his whiskered jaw. "No."

"Then your only alternative is to believe I'm insane."

"It has crossed my mind." He eyed her, thinking. "Or you've concocted a colorful story to deal with some bad shit in your past, and that's all right with me. Maybe the more times you tell the tale, the more I'll believe it."

"Since the night we met, I've given you hints. I've left bread-crumbs for you to follow to the reality of who, and what, I am. My problem with sunlight. My strength. My nomadic lifestyle. I heal quickly, and I don't injure easily. I can get into your head, as you said. What happened the night we met was your first clue. Why won't you take me seriously?"

"That was just rough fun and games. How about for now, let's just take this seriously."

Jax tossed his hat aside then smoothed his palms up and along her arms until his fingers reached the elastic neck of her peasant blouse neckline. He paused for the slightest moment to see if she'd stop him, but when she didn't, he drew the blouse off of her shoulders.

"Have you not wondered—really wondered—why I've kept you at an intimate distance since then? Jax, I bit you."

His hands stopped in his excursion to relieve her of her blouse, and he stared at her with the reality of what that meant finally getting through to him. "You. Bit. Me. And it didn't leave a mark." His rational mind sparred with the implausible possibility that everything she'd said was the god's honest truth.

Her eyebrows arched, and she nodded. "Now you're beginning to see those hints. You weren't supposed to remember what happened that night, but you did. My ability to trick your mind is a type of hypnotism that a vampire learns as a survival tactic. But it didn't work on you. That's never happened to me."

"So, I really did see two fangs against your bottom lip that night?"

That she didn't answer *was* the answer.

"Why did you deny it when I asked?"

"You don't believe me now that you know my life's story. You were even less likely to believe it then."

"You're hedging. There's another reason."

"Because... Because there was emotion involved. I cared about you." She placed her palm over his heart. "You, as a person, as a man I had feelings for. I didn't understand why, but it changed my intentions."

"What did you intend?" A shiver went down Jax's back.

"No. I wasn't going to kill you." Lissa smiled.

"Reading my thoughts again?"

"No, I see it in your eyes. Tough guy that you think you are, sometimes your emotions are transparent and give you away."

"What, then?"

"I was going to use you as a source of sustenance and sexual gratification. You had the kind of reputation I liked—a no strings attached relationship purely for mutual pleasure."

Jax pulled her blouse down a few more tantalizing, revealing inches. "There is one way to prove this to me."

"That is?"

"Show me your fangs. It'll go a long way toward my believing your story."

She shook her head and pulled up her blouse. "The feeding urge is powerful when they descend. I can control it, but I have yet to master it."

"You don't have to maintain control with me. Show me." He traced her lips with the tip of his index finger.

She grabbed his hand and jerked her head aside. "You still think this is a game. Just some bedtime story I've concocted for your amusement. Titillating foreplay."

"Well, I'll admit it's an enticing and intriguing story, but no one is immortal. Vampires are a Hollywood creation from Bram Stoker's—"

He didn't know how it happened. One moment he intended to kiss her, and the next he was flat on his back. Lissa squatted across his belly, her knees clamped against his sides, and her hands, like two iron grips on his biceps, held him down. Pinned to the ground, he looked into the blood-red sheen glowing in her eyes. Two pearly-white, glistening fangs rested against her bottom lip. He was as scared as he'd ever been.

"This is your only warning, Granger. Don't bully me, don't threaten me, and don't ever think you can dominate me."

The low, menacing promise in her voice sent ice surging through his veins. She bent toward him, her eyes holding him paralyzed with their mesmerizing glow.

"I am a vampire. I have witnessed the passing of centuries. I am immortal, and I will have your blood."

Her fangs sank into his neck; her lips burned like a red-hot brand pressed against his skin as she swallowed with the pulsing of his artery. How long she sucked, he didn't know. It might have been seconds or minutes. She moved around in his mind, laughing and taunting him, lording her power and strength over him, teaching him a lesson in humility. Then, abruptly, she released her grip. He watched, frozen, with a mixture of horror and awe as her fangs retracted, and she wiped a trickle of blood from the corner of her mouth. The red glow in her eyes returned to their normal color, and her mental hold on him dissolved. Slowly, he came back to himself.

Standing over him, she gazed down. "For your own good, leave, and don't come back. Forget me." She walked away.

A wave of stomach-turning dizziness hit Jax when he sat up. He held his head in his hands while gasping deep breaths until the urge to vomit passed. Grasping the back bumper and then the tailgate, Jax pulled himself to his feet and braced himself against the side of his pickup, his hands shaking and his heart pounding so hard he could hear it in his ears and feel it throbbing in his temples.

He tried to make sense of what happened. It wasn't real. Vampires were a myth, which meant Lissa really was batshit crazy delusional. Dangerous, even. His head told him to do as she said and leave, but his heart didn't listen. Whatever she was—vampire, human, or crazy—there was no living without her.

He pushed off from the fender, managing one shaky step after another until he made it to the house. Turning the handle, he gave the door a shove. He stood on the threshold, hands planted on both sides to brace himself on wobbly legs. Lissa stood in the middle of the room, her body a dark shadow in the candlelight.

"Did you turn me into a vampire?"

"No. That's a choice only you can make, and you'd have to take my blood for the turning to be complete and forever."

"You said you were dying when you made the choice. Is that a part of the process?"

"There are other ways but, generally, death is the precipitating event."

"Well, I'm not entertaining thoughts of dying any time soon."

"Jax, I left the human world for immortality, but that doesn't mean I shun the humanness I lost. I want what anyone wants—to live a satisfying life, to love, to be happy, to live. Do you know what you want?"

Her gaze, level and locked with his, bored into his heart, reaching down into the very core of his need and loneliness as a man who has no one to love. "Yeah. I do."

"What?"

"You."

In a dozen steps, he had her in his arms, his mouth on hers for the first honest kiss he'd ever given a woman—a kiss from his heart to hers—and he hoped like hell it curled her toes and butterflies were dive-bombing in her belly, because it was happening for him.

He rested his forehead on hers. "I want us to be together. A night. A week. Years. For the rest of my life—however long we have."

He sensed her thoughts in his head, probing and questioning, searching his feelings to read the truth of his words.

"You know what I am. I must have blood. I have no choice. I'll cease to exist. I'll die without it."

"I can deal with that."

"You say that now, but you have no idea what it means."

"Give me a chance to find out. Teach me. Don't expect me to forget about you. I can't. Don't say I have to go. And whatever you do, don't ever leave me."

"Someday, I will. Time will make it so."

He nodded. "But that time isn't now."

"You're right. That time isn't now." Backing up, she took his hand with a gentle tug. "We have this night."

Jax stood his ground. "I want more than just this night. Do you?"

She tugged his hand again. "Yes. But one night at a time is all we can have."

He went with her toward the bedroom. "Then that's all we need...for now."

A few weeks later, Jax finished disking-up the half-mile track at Lissa's place just ahead of the storm that moved in Thursday evening of Memorial Day weekend. Overnight, the track turned into a deep and muddy, sloppy mess, which was the exact condition he wanted for a mud-running excursion. Friday morning, he trailered-in four young horses and put them up in the rundown barn he'd been fixing up in his spare time.

During an afternoon break in the rain, Jax asked Lissa to help him with the horses. They took two of the colts for a gallop then returned them to the barn and saddled the other two. When Jax swung up to the back of his salty two-year-old gelding, he knew right off he had his hands full. The gelding balked at the mud, which made it a chore to finish one trip around the track even with Lissa and her filly along as company. As hardheaded as the horse, Jax wasn't about to let the gelding get the better of him. No horse ever had.

"Lissa, I'm taking this fella a couple more rounds by himself. He's as barn-sour as he is buddy-sour."

"All right. I'll put this girl up and set out the hay and grain. It's a little early for evening chores, but it feels like it's about to rain again."

"Good idea. We won't be long."

When Lissa cut off at the gap to head for the barn, Jax expected his horse would naturally follow, and he was right. Plow-reining him, Jax made the gelding continue alone. The horse cut back twice, but Jax brought him around each time, and they made it around the track at a slow jog without trouble. It was a different story when they passed the fence gap the second time. The colt fought against Jax's insistence to keep going, tossing his head left and right to break Jax's hold on the reins. When that got him nowhere, he wheeled and started backing up. Jax knew from experience what was coming. The horse tensed; Jax kicked free of the stirrups. The colt's front legs bounced against the ground twice, then his front end lifted as he threw himself over backward.

"You little son of a bi—"

Jax bailed off just as the colt slipped in the mud and came crashing down, his massive shoulder smashing Jax's chest when they hit the ground. In the colt's mad, thrashing scramble to regain his footing, a flailing aluminum stirrup sliced the brachial artery in Jax's left arm.

Jax tried to push upright, but his body failed him. Nothing worked right, and his left arm was useless. He sank into the mud, working hard to catch his breath. Determined, he made it to his knees with his right hand planted on the ground for support. Staring down at his blood-soaked clothes, his mind didn't grasp that it was his blood. No one could lose that much blood so fast and live. Then the reality of his mortality hit him. Pain burned through his body. His vision blurred, and the cloudy sky heaved and twisted in a weird vertigo dance.

Lying there, he remembered all the times Steve told him these damned horses would kill him someday. He tried to laugh, but a bloody, bubbling coughing was all he could manage. Closing his eyes, he wished he'd have told Lissa what she meant to him. He should have said the words. He should have told her he loved her. He wondered if she loved him. He wished he'd heard her say it...

Chapter Nine

"Jax! Jax! Open your eyes!"

Lissa ripped his goggles away from his face. He blinked, felt pressure on his arm. He tried his best to smile. She'd found him. It was good not to die alone.

"No no no no no! Come back!"

He jerked awake. Didn't she know how tired he was? He just wanted to sleep.

"Talk to me! Jax. Don't you give up!"

Talk? He knew what he wanted to say, but there was a lag between thought and speech. "Am I...dead?"

"No, but you don't have long. I've got pressure above the cut, but the bleeding won't stop."

The sob in her voice brought him back with a surge of strength from the brink of too far gone.

"I... cast the stones... yesterday and... and this morning." He patted his jean's pocket. "In here. This one..."

"There's no time. Please, Jax, I can't lose you. I can save you, but you have to make the choice."

"Get it... Get the stone."

Lissa dug into his pocket and held the stone where he could see it. "It's Fire."

He rasped the words, "Fire destroys... Creates."

"Transformation."

"Red. Blood. Blood of life." He made a feeble gesture at his bloody arm, then touched her face with his fingertips for a fleeting moment before the weight of his arm was too much to bear up.

"Jax, you have to say it. Tell me you want to live."

With a weak nod, he wheezed, "Save me. Save me for us."

A host of sensations swirled in his fading consciousness: his sleeve ripping, Lissa's mouth pressed on his arm, thunder rumbling in the distance as if the storm was angry with the day. A lightness of mind and soul filled him. Peace replaced pain, and his head lolled to the side.

A stinging slap on his face pulled him from his stupor.

"Jax! Open your eyes. You have to take my blood now. Do you hear me? Damn it! Open your eyes now!"

She hovered over him, her face blurry and distorted, but he saw a blade on her pocket knife clearly enough. She pressed the edge to her neck, her hand poised to make the slice. The peaceful comfort of death vanished with a cold, hollow emptiness taking its place. His will to live rushed back in waves of bone-deep, agonizing pain.

"Give me... Give me tomorrow."

Lissa sliced her carotid artery then gathered him into her arms, cradling him so her blood dripped onto his lips.

"Swallow. Take all you can, or you'll die a mortal death."

He tasted the sharp coppery-salty tang on his tongue. His mind resisted but, somehow, he pushed past his gag reflex to put his mouth against her neck and swallow time and again. From somewhere separate from his body, he watched himself—repulsed yet unable to stop—take Lissa's life-giving blood into his mouth.

Darkness engulfed him. He tumbled weightless into the vast unknown beyond life. His heart made its final beat, and he spiraled into the pitch-black nothingness of nothing.

Jax's dead weight pushed Lissa deeper into the cushion of mud. Eyes closed, she felt a gust of breeze and cool spattering sprinkles wetting her face. She wanted to sleep. Sleep for days and days. She felt drained—literally and figuratively—but there was no time to dally. She had to get them both inside.

With mechanical movements, she felt Jax's neck for a pulse. Rapid and erratic, but strong, just as she'd hoped. His transformation was underway. Despite the low, heavy cloud cover, it wasn't safe for either of them to remain outside in their weakened condition. Even muted light was their enemy, and direct sunlight would kill them. She was already feeling the prickling needles of sunburn on the back of her neck and tops of her ears as well as across her cheeks. A darkened environment was their only refuge while they rested and regenerated.

Pushing Jax off of her, she grabbed a handful of his shirt to help pull herself to her knees. She tottered to her feet, assuming a wide-legged stance to keep her balance. For many seconds, she stared down at him. How was she going to get him to the house? He was a big guy. She ran through options and came up short. A vehicle would get mired down; calling for emergency responders was out of the question. She could drag him, but even that—

Lightning flashed on an immediate boom of thunder. Lissa went to one knee in an instinctive duck. The hairs on her arms stood up and the skin on the backs of her gloveless hands turned red like they were scalded with steam. Without thinking about the impossibility, she grabbed Jax's hands and heaved him up and across her shoulders in a fireman's carry. Gritting her teeth, a low, guttural, growling groan rose from her chest as she stood under his weight. Staggering, willing her legs not to give out, she lumbered toward the house one leaden footstep at a time. She went to her knees twice, but another flash of too-close lightning and a sudden cloudburst brought the rush of adrenaline she needed to make it the last few yards to the back door.

Her intent, as she shuffled through the kitchen and into the living room, was to put Jax on the sofa, but his weight and her weakness dumped them both on the floor shy of her mark. Many minutes passed before her legs recovered sufficiently to take her outside to put up Jax's colt.

Slogging through the mud, she made it to the barn, found the colt pacing at the doors, and put him inside with the other three. A cursory check as she removed his saddle and bridle revealed no serious injuries. Halfway back to the house, a frigid gust of wind hit her broadside, which meant one thing. *Hail!* She took off running. She lurched through the kitchen door and slammed it shut an instant before the wall of wind-driven hail blasted the house. Her back against the door, her entire being numb and weakened, darkness crept into her mind. The healing tonic of sleep beckoned, but checking on Jax and then taking a long, hot shower to wash off the blood and grime came first. Pushing off from the closed door, she took a couple of steps when her legs folded. Out cold on the kitchen floor was as far as she got.

Light. A tiny pinpoint of flickering light. A beacon guiding him to shore on the inky, black sea surrounding him.

Jax fixed his gaze on that light with the determination of a drowning man clutching a life buoy. Slowly, his mind cleared, and questions emerged. Where was he? How did he get here? Shifting position, he realized he was lying on a sofa with a blanket over him and a pillow under his head. He squinted to identify the dark, shadowy objects in the room.

"There's water to your right. The lemon juice in it will refresh you."

Lissa! He turned his head toward the sound of her voice.

"Drink all you can to rehydrate. It will lessen the headache that's going to hit you like an ax stroke between your eyes the first time you sit up. I called Steve and told him you had food poisoning and you'd stay here until you recovered. He doesn't expect you for a few days."

"How long—" He coughed to clear the sticky dryness in his throat. "How long was I out?" He fumbled for the water and gulped the glass dry.

"Since late Friday afternoon. It's Monday night." Lissa came into the candlelight and refilled the water glass. "I cleaned you up and washed your clothes. I mended your shirtsleeve and put a bandage on your arm."

He croaked out, "Thanks."

"What do you remember?"

Resting back on the pillow, he went through his memories. He recalled the colt throwing himself backward and the fall, then the pain. Taking Lissa's life-giving blood was a blur that faded into an elusive memory of floating in a dark void of nothingness.

"All of it up to when I blacked out. How'd you get me to the house?"

"With difficulty. Six feet of solid muscle is no picnic to move by yourself."

Chuckling sent a sharp pain spiking through his chest. "Damn. I feel like I was hit by a freight train."

"You were. That colt has some meat on his shoulders. He came down on you with his full weight."

"I remember. Is he okay?"

"Yes. Scratched up and undoubtedly sore, but no permanent damage. You, on the other hand, sustained broken ribs and a crushed chest. But you're healing rapidly. In a few days, you won't have any physical indications. I've never encountered anyone with your healing metabolism."

Jax rubbed his bicep, flexing his fingers and extending his arm to test mobility, and found the pain of a deep, healing cut and the soreness of a pulled muscle. "I guess this means what you did for me worked. I'm, ah, like you. I'm a..." He felt funny saying the word. "Vampire"

"Yes, although a fledgling vampire with exceptional resilience. I didn't fully awaken for two weeks after my turning. It took many more weeks for my burns to heal and the scars to disappear. In fact, even after all this time, I still have telltale signs of scars on my back. I realize the extent of my burns was considerably worse than your injuries, but you're rapidly mending. It's amazing. No. It's extraordinary."

"How can that happen? How can our bodies heal when we're essentially dead?"

Lissa sat on the edge of the sofa beside him and refilled his glass again. "We're not technically dead. We're regenerated.

We've adapted. We still possess the essence of what it means to be human, and our bodies continue to function as such. We still require sleep, although we prefer to sleep when it's light outside. We eat and drink, albeit with altered tastes and nutritional requirements. We desire the same material comforts we did before. We have the same fears and joys, hopes and dreams. We love. We grieve. We wish, and we regret."

"Do vampires have families? How does that work?

Lissa remained silent.

"Touchy subject?"

"No. It's difficult to explain."

"I'm not going anywhere soon. Tell me. I need to know these things."

"Yes, I suppose you do. We've adapted and evolved in order to survive and integrate into society. To do otherwise means suicide by extinction."

"But—"

"But barrenness is a price that comes with the transformation, which isn't to say there are no children born to vampires. Pregnancy rarely happens, and then only when the couple has exceptional metabolism and resilience. It's quite a celebrated event when a vampire baby is born. There have been instances of pregnant women undergoing the transformation and both mother and child survive. All vampire-blooded children, whether transformed in the womb, which is rare, or born in the natural course of events, will mature as a human until age twenty or so, when the turning naturally completes."

"That's incredible. Go back to the altered nutritional requirements. How do we handle the whole needing blood situation?"

"Fresh human blood is most satisfying and nutritious, but any blood will suffice. Animal blood is an acquired taste, but readily available if you work in an animal-related profession."

"You bite animals for their blood." He grimaced. "I don't think I can do that. For that matter, I don't think I can bite a human for their blood, either."

"You'll find that biting to sate blood hunger isn't necessary, but the downside is it's powerfully instinctual to bite. Controlling the biting urge will be the first challenge you'll face. You'll always struggle to keep it in its place."

"That doesn't answer my question. How do we get the blood without biting?"

"I rarely take human blood. I extract a few CCs with needle and syringe from horses once a week. You'll require several times that for many years, before your body adjusts to surviving on a lesser amount."

Jax swallowed hard. "Talking about this is like trying to swallow a raw egg. Gets me right here." He placed the tips of his fingers on the sides of his neck just below his earlobes.

Lissa nodded, smiling. "I understand. I've been there, too. You'll overcome your aversion when the blood craving is burning in your body."

"That doesn't sound like much fun."

"It's not but, as I said, you'll adapt, or you'll die. And by die, I mean you'll either starve, or you'll do something that gets you involved with the legal system. An incarcerated or institutionalized vampire is a frightening thing to see."

Blowing out a hard breath, he asked, "Now what?"

"It's a new world for you, and a new life awaits. Your education begins, and I'm your teacher."

Nodding slowly, Jax said, "Sure as hell hope I'm a fast learner."

"What do you mean, I can't work outside like I used to? You do. I've got a hat, gloves, and long sleeves. I'll slather on a gallon or two of sun-blocking lotion. I'll be okay."

"I've been a vampire for centuries. I've grown and matured in my tolerance to sunlight. You'll have to test your own resistance and manage your life around how much sunlight you can bear, or you'll fry. Literally. With your metabolism, you'll probably get along being out in the daytime for short periods of time, if you take frequent advantage of shaded areas. Overcast days will be your best friend, but even then, you can't overdo it. You'll just have to test your tolerance with experimentation."

"Damn it!" Jax slammed his coffee cup on the counter. "This is what happens when you don't read the fine print."

Lissa faced him, her eyes hard, her jaw set. "I didn't force you. You made the choice to turn. It will get easier with time."

"Yeah. In a few hundred years. Shit." He ran his fingers through his hair in frustration. "Shit."

"Your alternative was mortal death."

Drawing in a breath, he blew it out in a slow, hard exhale, his exasperation lessening with the reminder. "I know. I know."

"It's natural to be angry. I was."

"For how long? Honestly."

"Honestly? I still am. Intellectually, I've accepted my choice, but I have yet to come to terms with it emotionally. Up until I met you, I'd only used humans for occasional physical companionship and as sustenance when other means of acquiring blood weren't available or feasible."

"Great. Just great. We're vampires in existential crisis. Now there's some irony for you."

"You're in the transition phase. It's turmoil hell. You can fight it, or you can figure out how to deal with it. Either way, it's part of who you are now. You can't avoid it. I'll guide you. I'll encourage you. But you have to make the adjustments on your own. There are no shortcuts."

"I haven't been to the ranch in five days. It's sundown." He grabbed his hat. "I'm hauling the horses home. I'll talk to you later." The windows shook when the door slammed.

Lissa let him go. He needed distance between them. She understood that. Right now, he was as beholden to her as he was angry and conflicted. She remembered her inner turmoil in the months immediately after her turning all too well. Hating who she was. Angry at the dirty trick life had played on her. Wishing it hadn't happened. Yet, somehow, throughout the years, a tiny spark of hope remained in her heart as a reminder that the essence of herself, her human soul, was still a part of her and could never be taken away. It was what she clung to, what gave her life meaning, what kept her going. Jax would find it, too. He just needed time. And time was something they both had plenty of.

A vampire sanctuary was where he should be right now, sheltered from the world of humans where he could explore his new 'self', create a new identity, learn to master the blood cravings where he wouldn't get himself into trouble or hurt anyone until he figured out how to navigate his new life.

But Jax was Jax. He'd come to grips with his situation, or he wouldn't. She could only offer guidance when he'd accept it and moral support whether he wanted it or not. What she did know with complete surety was he'd succumb to his bloodlust despite his naïve confidence that it would never happen to him. Then, and only then, would he understand the power he possessed over humans and the responsibility of keeping it, and himself, under control.

But, more than that, she hoped when he stepped over the line of no return, he wouldn't hate her for turning him.

Chapter Ten

"I killed her. She's dead. Lissa. She's dead."

"Who's dead?"

Silence.

"Jax! Who's dead?" Lissa gripped the telephone. She held her breath, and the sick feeling in the pit of her stomach worsened. She knew what he wasn't saying. She'd watched it build every day since his turning not yet six months ago. She warned him his confidence in his self-control would turn on him, but he brushed her off.

"Allison."

"Where are you?" A glance at the time. Nine-thirty.

"My house. I couldn't help myself. I need you here. Now!"

Lissa made a white-knuckle drive from the vet clinic where she was catching up on paperwork. She skidded to a stop in front of Jax's house in a shower of gravel. Bursting through the kitchen door and on into the living room, she saw in a glance what had transpired—a half-empty whiskey bottle and two glasses on the coffee table, unconscious woman on the couch and Jax pacing like a trapped tiger in front of the fireplace.

Kneeling beside the woman, Lissa felt for her pulse. Strong and rapid. The two puncture marks on her neck were closing up.

Lissa stepped into Jax's path and grabbed him by the shoulders. "She's not dead, but you certainly did a number on her."

Jax's eyes shone with the wide, pupil-dilated sheen of an animal backed into a corner. He was wired and in ultra-alert mode. His gaze darted between Allison and Lissa.

"I bit her. I bit her." Jax looked at her as if hoping to find an answer to a question he didn't understand.

"Who is she?"

"She's a jockey. I've known her for years. We couldn't seem to get along for more than a few weeks at a stretch. If there was ever a woman I would have—"

He didn't finish, but Lissa knew what he meant.

"I understand. She's your friend, and we'll treat her as such."

"I'm ashamed to admit that I came up short in the friend department with her. Why she kept coming back after I hurt her...used her..." He shook his head. "She came here tonight to tell me she's met a man—a trainer—and he wants to settle down and have a family. She's getting married. She was in Denver to tell her family in person. She went out of her way to drive here to tell me." He watched her for several moments. "I meant more to her than she ever did to me. I'm sorry about that. I'm sorry I've hurt her that way. But I'm glad her life is going someplace that makes her happy." A deep scowl wrinkled his forehead. "I cooked supper. We had a few drinks. We talked." His frown deepened. "Then we said goodbye, and she hugged me, and...and...the next thing I knew..."

His knees buckled. Lissa caught him and backed him to the edge of the coffee table. "Sit down before you fall down."

"I'm burning up inside. Dizzy. My head feels like it's going to explode. I can't catch my breath." Teeth gritted, he rubbed the heel of his hand across his chest.

"You're on a feeding high. You took too much blood from her. It will happen until you learn to regulate your cravings. You only need a few ounces at a time, and you don't have to feed by biting. You know that."

"You're saying it's like a sugar high from eating all the Halloween candy in one sitting." He tried to laugh.

"Or caffeine overload from drinking too many pots of coffee."

"My mouth is killing me. I feel like a mule kicked me in the face with both hind feet."

"The pain of fangs descending and retracting is brutal. That's one reason we find other sources of blood than biting. It hurts like holy hell. Every. Single. Time. Although, the first time is the worst—as you just discovered."

"Why the hell didn't you warn me?" Jax dug his fist against his mouth.

"I didn't tell you on purpose. You had to experience it stone cold, so you'd never forget what the first time feels like. Remembered pain helps temper and control your urge to bite. Now stay put while I fix things up here."

Lissa took the whiskey bottle to the kitchen and poured out all but an inch. She rummaged through the cupboards for more alcohol, found his stash, and went through the same pouring-out routine with the tequila. She took two shot glasses and the tequila and returned to the living room. On the coffee table, she tipped over a whiskey glass look like it had spilled, poured a swallow or two into the other whiskey glass, and arranged the bottle of tequila and shot glasses on the table. She removed Allison's shoes then shook out the afghan blanket from the back of the couch and draped it over her.

"All right. Here's your story. You two reminisced about old times, had a few laughs, shared racetrack stories, and drank too much booze. Time got away from you. She passed out. You called me to come help, because you were too drunk to take care of her. She'll wake up with a doozy of a hangover. She'll feel lousy for several days, but she won't remember much, if anything, leading up to the bite or that you fed on her. She'll simply attribute how rotten she feels to a hangover. You are going to perpetuate that lie, which should be easy, because you'll have the same hangover."

"I can do that."

"I'll stay and watch over both of you. In your condition, you're in no shape to handle her reaction when she wakes up. I'll run interference. I want her to leave here with her dignity and self-respect intact."

Jax managed a nodding thank you.

"Come on." Lissa got her shoulder under Jax's arm and hauled him to his feet. "You've got to drink some water and then sleep this off. It's all that will help."

Jax glanced back at Allison when they reached the bedroom door. "She'll be all right?"

"Yes, but it'll be hours before she wakes."

Jax collapsed onto the bed and Lissa pulled off his boots, unable to resist a good scolding stemming from an all too real fear for what he'd done.

"Jax. Listen to me. You're new to this. You have to moderate your bloodthirst, or your cravings will always rule your judgment. You'll kill someone and, believe me, you don't want that on your conscience. Besides, it isn't necessary. It takes self--discipline and practice without which you endanger yourself and risk exposure for what you really are. Humans can't know about us, or our existence will end and—"

He was out cold. He hadn't heard a word.

On a tired sigh, Lissa rubbed her hands over her face. Up to now, he'd not taken blood by physical means. She'd sheltered him from that method of sating his blood-hunger through teaching him other methods of extracting and ingesting blood. But, now that he'd bitten a human, had literally gotten a taste of fresh, human blood, he was in a new phase of his trans-formation. Until he mastered himself and his cravings, he was in danger of harming other people he cared about. Difficult decisions lay before him now.

While she'd gotten used to her nomadic lifestyle and, since the turn of the century, it had gotten easier to integrate into human society as well as to disappear well ahead of *Grab your torch and pitchforks!* when she'd stayed too long in one place, she still felt the heartache of leaving friends behind knowing with each move she'd likely never see them again.

She watched Jax for a few seconds. He had yet to feel the pain and heartache of leaving loved ones. A little pang of sorrow tugged at her heart. She didn't wish that on anyone. But wishing didn't change reality.

Snuggling in beside him to rest for a few hours, Lissa closed her eyes. A line from Macbeth flitted through her thoughts as she drifted off.

Life's but a walking shadow, a poor player that struts and frets his hour upon the stage and then is heard no more.

❦

Daylight pinked on the horizon as Lissa sat at the kitchen island counter with a freshly brewed cup of coffee while listening to Allison's waking up noises.

"Jax?" Allison mumbled. "Jax. Are you here?" Her voice gained strength when she sat up.

Lissa filled a mug with coffee, squeezed a thick slice of lemon into a glass of water, and took them to the living room. "Here. This will make you feel better. Drink the water first." She handed the water to Allison and placed the mug on the coffee table.

"Thank you." Allison took the water and drank it all despite the squinting grimace of the tart lemon taste, then she traded empty glass for hot coffee. As she sipped from the mug, her gaze fell on the array of bottles and glasses on the coffee table. "For as rotten as I feel, we must have had a good time."

Lissa nodded, but didn't comment. She sat in a chair near Allison and waited.

"Is Jax here?"

"Yes. He's passed out in the bedroom."

The time it took Allison to process that tiny bit of information said much about her headache and fuzzy memories.

"Who are you?"

"Lissa Price."

"You're a friend of Jax's?"

"Yes."

"Close friend...as in romantic?"

Lissa saw questions igniting in Allison's eyes, and she headed them off with a soft, understanding smile and simple explanation. "We're good friends, and I'm also his veterinarian. He trusts me. He called to have me watch over both of you. He was too drunk to take care of himself, but he did have enough sense to know you'd also had too much to drink."

Allison's deep frown indicated she still couldn't wrap her memories around last night, but she didn't want to admit the extent of her alcohol-induced amnesia.

"He cares about you. Quite a lot, in fact."

"Did he actually say that?"

"Yes. He also said you're getting married. He hopes you have a wonderfully happy life."

Allison smiled. "I've loved him since... I think since the first time I met him, many years ago. But Jax is Jax. Emotionally untouchable. He's the bad boy a girl wants to have a fling with but, in the end, he's not the guy a girl should set her sights on marrying. Although, I think there was a time last winter when we could have made it together if he'd have let himself admit he loved me. Funny how things turn out. He finally broke my heart one too many times, and I was able to let go of him and open my heart to someone else. I came here to tell him that."

"Caring for Jax is risky, and he has a way about him that doesn't always bring out the best in people."

Allison's giggle came on a grimace at the pain it caused in her hung-over head. "Isn't that the truth?"

She finished the coffee in silence, alternately sipping and closing her eyes while leaning her head back on the couch. On a resigned sigh, she threw off the afghan and gathered her shoes.

"It's daylight. I'd better go. If I leave now, I'll be in Denver by breakfast. Maybe I won't be in too much trouble for making everyone worry that I didn't return last night." Hastily, she added, "I'm not a little girl, and I do what I want, but..."

"Your fiancé?"

"You're perceptive."

"Did you tell him you were coming to see Jax?"

"Yes."

"Then he trusts you, so trust him to honor your independence and integrity. If he doesn't, then he's not worth having. Do you have a cell phone?"

"I do."

"If he was worried, he could have called. But, if doubts crop up, call me." Lissa found a pen and paper in end table drawer and wrote her number for Allison. "But call him and let him know you're on your way."

Allison stood on wobbly legs, got her balance, and walked to Jax's bedroom. She didn't stay long. "I couldn't wake him. When you talk to him, please tell him goodbye for me."

Lissa nodded. "I will."

Allison located her purse and jacket and closed the kitchen door quietly behind her.

Lissa poured another cup of coffee and went out to the deck to watch the sunrise. Two hours later, Jax stumbled to the kitchen door.

"When did Allison leave?"

"Daylight."

"Is she okay? Does she hate me?"

"Yes and no. She made peace with you and put her feelings in a safe place. But she deserves an apology for last night, and also for how you've treated her in the past."

"I know."

"Plane tickets to Hawaii would make a nice apology."

"Good idea."

"Don't leave her hanging."

"I won't. I'll take care of it later. I'm going back to bed."

Lissa lingered outside for a few more minutes, then she followed him.

"Join me?" Jax lifted the bedspread.

Lissa slipped off her boots and got under the covers with him. He pulled her close and she rested her head on his shoulder. She sensed he had something to say, so she remained quiet while he worked it out in his mind.

"Tell me that vampire creation story you like."

"All right. It begins with a young Italian man named Ambrogio. All his life, he yearned to visit the Oracle of Delphi to have his future told. When he was old enough to travel on his own, he sailed to Greece and made his way to Delphi which, if you recall, was also the home of Apollo's great sun temple. When Ambrogio reached the temple and approached the Pythia, she spoke these cryptic words: 'The curse. The moon. The blood will run.' Ambrogio stewed over the meaning throughout the night. When daylight arrived, he encountered a beautiful woman dressed in white robes walking toward the temple. He introduced himself. Her name was Selene."

"Moon."

"Yes. She was a temple maiden, and her sister was the Oracle. Selene tended the temple and watched over her sister when she was entranced."

"I'll bet Ambrogio and Selene fell in love and all sorts of trouble followed."

"It did. On his last day in Greece, Ambrogio asked Selene to marry him and return to Italy with him in the morning. She said yes. Unbeknownst to them, Apollo had been watching their activity, and he was furious that a mortal would dare lure away one of his temple maidens. You know how those gods are."

Jax nodded, chuckling.

"At sunset, Apollo appeared to Ambrogio and placed a curse on him that sunlight would forever burn Ambrogio's skin. So, unable to meet Selene at daylight as planned, Ambrogio appealed to Hades for help. Hades made a deal with Ambrogio that if he stole Artemis's silver bow and brought it to him, Hades would provide protection in the Underworld for Ambrogio and Selene."

"They'd better watch out. There's always a kicker with Hades."

"It's a doozy. Hades gave Ambrogio a magical wooden bow and 11 arrows to hunt with. Ambrogio was to offer his hunting trophies to Artemis, which would gain him her favor, and then he could steal her silver bow and bring it to Hades. But, as you said, the kicker was Ambrogio had to leave his soul with Hades as collateral."

"And something went wrong."

"Yes. That something happened when Ambrogio killed a swan with one of the magic arrows. He used its feathers as pens to dip into the swan's blood as ink, so he could write a message on a piece of parchment to Selene to tell her what had happened. Although upset at this turn of events, Selene continued her daily duties at the temple. The second day, she found a love poem Ambrogio had written, in blood, for her. This note-writing went on for forty-four days. Finally, Ambrogio offered a dead swan to Artemis. If you recall, she is Apollo's twin sister."

"The plot thickens."

"Ambrogio reasoned that even if he couldn't steal the silver bow, maybe Artemis would accept the swan as tribute and convince Apollo to lift the curse. On the forty-fifth night, Ambrogio had only one arrow left, and he missed his shot at another swan, and therefore the ability to write another love note to Selene. His dreams of being reunited with Selene were gone. He wept. But Artemis had been watching. She admired his dedication to her and his skill as a hunter, so she came to him and agreed to let him borrow her silver bow and one arrow to kill one last bird so he could write his farewell to Selene."

"No doubt, he went back on his word."

"He did. As he ran to Hades to give him the silver bow and arrows, Artemis cast her own curse on Ambrogio to stop him. Her curse made all silver burn his skin. Well, he told his sad story to Artemis, and she took pity on him. She granted him one more chance. Her deal was, she'd make him into a great hunter with god-like speed and strength along with fangs for draining the blood of beasts in order to write his notes to Selene. However, in order to gain this immortality, he and Selene had to escape from Apollo's temple and swear to worship Artemis forever.

"Now, another twist to this story is Artemis was a virgin goddess. Only the chaste and unmarried could follow her. If Ambrogio accepted her deal, he could never touch Selene again. Not a kiss. Nothing. No children. Well, Ambrogio said yes. He and Selene would be together, albeit, platonically, and that was enough for him. So he killed another swan, wrote a note with instructions for what she should do, and she managed to flee the temple before Apollo figured out what had happened."

"I've got a bad feeling about this."

"Actually, it has a happy ending— Well, as happy as any Greek myth can end. Selene located Ambrogio's ship at the dock, and she searched until she found a wooden coffin in the hull. The note on the coffin instructed her to tell the captain to set sail and for her to wait until after sundown to open the coffin. She did both, and she was reunited with Ambrogio who emerged from the coffin quite alive and well.

"They made their home in Ephesus in a cave during the day and at night, they worshipped Artemis with all their heart. They passed the years together, never touching, never kissing, and never having children. When Selene reached the end of her mortal life, Ambrogio couldn't bear to live on forever without her, so he killed a white swan, offered it to Artemis, and begged her to make Selene immortal.

"Artemis rewarded their years of dedication and worship and allowed Ambrogio to touch Selene just once in order to drink blood. This act would kill her mortal body and, from that moment on, their mixed blood would create eternal life for anyone who drank it. Ambrogio was reluctant, but Selene encouraged him. He bit her neck, took her blood into his body, and in that moment of transformation between death and rebirth, Selene radiated a brilliant light that rose to the sky and her spirit lifted to meet Artemis at the moon."

"So that's how Selene became the goddess of moonlight."

"It is, and every night she reaches down with her light to touch Ambrogio and all of her children."

"What children?"

"Vampires who carry the blood of Ambrogio and Selene."

Jax nodded with a soft smile. "I should have seen that coming. That's a nice story in a bittersweet sort of way."

"It is a nice story. It reaches me in a place that makes me feel better about who, and what, I am."

"Yeah. Makes me feel better, too."

Jax fell silent for some time, and Lissa was content to just be near and lost in her own thoughts.

"We've talked about leaving here, but never seriously. It's time to make those decisions, isn't it?" Jax tilted his head back to see her face.

"Yes. It is."

"We could go on the road with the transport service. I could keep in touch with my family from a safe distance. Still be a part of them. I'd like to see Steve and Mandy's kids while they're growing up."

Lissa nodded that she understood. "So would I. We can also work on night-running tracks. Tracks don't turn veterinarians away."

"I've worked as a gateman and as a farrier."

"You could do more sketches and sell them, too."

"Sounds like the backside of the racetrack is the perfect place for us."

"If it doesn't work out, there are sanctuaries where we can disappear at any time and for as long as we need."

"Life sure has a way of throwing curve balls into a person's plans. Dad will retire in a year or two now that he and Mom are remarried. They've talked about moving back here. Wanting to be close to three little grandkids no doubt influenced that decision." Jax stared at the ceiling. "Do we have to leave right away?"

"Not as long as you take better care to manage your cravings and not succumb to physically feeding on humans. We can continue living and working here until people notice we're not aging as they are. We'll have no choice but to leave when that happens. It's best to leave before that happens"

"The price of immortality is saying goodbye forever and then living that forever without the people you care about."

"Yes. And unfortunately, that time will come long before you're ready."

Jax looked at her. "For everyone's sake to be safe from me, I think we'd better leave while I get this vampirism figured out."

Lissa propped on an elbow. "That's a wise decision. You can tell your friends and family we're going to travel and see the world. You can say you're having a mid-life crisis at thirty-seven."

He grunted. "That's for damn sure." He was quiet for a few moments. "Have you ever killed anyone?"

Lissa heard what he didn't say—the realization and fear of how close he'd come to killing Allison.

"No, but I've had close calls that I'm not proud of, and I've witnessed feedings gone wrong. The primal urge to survive at the expense of another's life is a horrible guilt I hope you never have to bear."

A slow smile softened his serious frown. "All right. Then let's make this a helluva going away party. If I have to leave town, I want my own parade." He pulled her over to lay prone upon him. "How long has it been since you heard the words 'I love you'?"

Her breath hitched, and an instant of misty emotion filled her eyes. "A long time. A really, really, really long time. Why?"

His devilish grin widened. "Because I love you, Melissa Price, and I won't wait a really, really, really long time to say it again." He placed a light kiss on her lips.

"I love you, Jaxon Granger." Hearing those words and uttering them herself lifted the lonely weight of the years from her heart.

"And to think this all started with an injured horse, a dream, a few pencil scratchings, and a little rock with squiggly lines on it."

"Yes, it did."

"Do vampires get married?"

"Is this a proposal?"

"Yep, and I'll even spring for a diamond ring to prove it."

Lissa laughed. "Well, aren't you Mr. Romantic all of a sudden?"

"You didn't answer me. Do vampires get married?"

"Of course."

"Then that's the parade I want. Damn the expense. I want a full-blown dog-and-pony-show black tie affair wedding with a reception and dance that lasts until dawn on the winter solstice. We'll get married at sundown on the longest night of the year. Then we'll take off to travel the world on our honeymoon. Forever."

"Forever. I like that. Until this moment, forever was a word I dreaded."

"So that's a yes to my proposal?"

"Yes, it's a yes." Lissa giggled.

Jax laughed with her. "Good. Now, I have a request."

Lissa arched her eyebrows. "What's that?"

"I want to meet Lord Burton and thank him."

"Thank him for what?"

"For giving you tomorrow so you could give it to me."

"I can arrange that meeting. He'll be pleased and honored to meet you. In fact, he'll probably invite us to stay with him for a hundred years or so."

Jax chuckled. "A century of hospitality. Who could say no to that?"

"Now it's my turn to ask something of you."

"Okay. Ask away. Anything you want."

Grinning slyly, Lissa leaned down and brushed a warm kiss across Jax's lips. "Make me late for work."

About the Author

Native Coloradoan Kaye Spencer grew up on a cattle ranch in northeastern Colorado. Since 1990, she's lived in a small, rural town located in the heart of the infamous Dust Bowl area of the 1930s in southeastern Colorado. Kaye writes mostly western romances.

Louis L'Amour's western novels, Marty Robbins' gunfighter ballads, and western movies and tv shows inspired her love of the American Old West—truths and myths alike. Kaye's favorite movie line is from 'Quigley Down Under': "I said I never had much use for one. Never said I didn't know how to use it." (This is exactly her relationship with her kitchen.)

During Kaye's younger years, she followed the amateur rodeo circuit and experienced life on the thoroughbred racetrack. She even did a stint as a cleaner of sugar beet storage silos (after beets are processed into sugar) to keep down the sugar dust in order to minimize static electricity. Otherwise... BOOM! As a single mother, she did manage to find less-explosive jobs to support herself and her three young children.

Having had enough of 'odd' jobs, Kaye entered college to earn a B.A. in teaching. The degree landed her a position as librarian for a 90,000-volume children's library. After that, she returned to college for her M.A. From there, she worked as a teacher of students with special needs, school psychologist, 6th– 12th grades English and history teacher, principal, and director of exceptional student services. Some thirty-five years later, she retired. She is fortunate to be able to spend a lot of time with her family. Many rescued and homeless animals have found a home with her, and more are always welcome.

Learn more about Kaye, her books, and where to find her on social media. Her website is www.kayespencer.com

Also by

Give My Love to Rose – The Comanchero's Bride
Curse of the Brystile Witch – Gunfighters & Ghostriders

www.ingramcontent.com/pod-product-compliance
Lightning Source LLC
Chambersburg PA
CBHW060741180626
46819CB00001B/59